W9-BGL-067

12-16-11
12-18-15

Luke Sutton:
Hired Gun

by Leo P. Kelley

Luke Sutton: Hired Gun

LEO P. KELLEY

DOUBLEDAY & COMPANY, INC.

GARDEN CITY, NEW YORK

1987

All of the characters in this book
are fictitious, and any resemblance
to actual persons, living or dead,
is purely coincidental.

Library of Congress Cataloging-in-Publication Data

Kelley, Leo P.
Luke Sutton, hired gun.

I. Title.
PS3561.E388L834   1987   813'.54   87-624
ISBN: 0-385-23787-1

Luke Sutton:
Hired Gun

ONE

The barber beckoned, his big blue eyes twinkling, as Luke Sutton strode into the man's shop.

"Over here, Luke," he said, still beckoning, his eyes still twinkling. "I've something to show you."

Sutton followed the barber over to the mug-filled rack that hung on and nearly completely covered one wall of the shop. He studied the mugs for a moment before asking, "What is it you want to show me, Dennis?"

With a dramatic flourish, Dennis removed a white china mug from the small square cubicle it occupied on the rack. With another flourish and a slight bow he presented it to Sutton.

"Well now," Sutton murmured softly, looking down at the mug that bore his name in ornate gold letters. "I'd never expected to have my own personal mug in a barbershop, Dennis. I'm surprised. And honored."

"You ought not to be surprised, Luke," Dennis declared amiably. "You're well known and well respected here in Virginia City. Why, you've become about as much of a town fixture as Doctor Senlow—Dennis indicated a mug bearing the doctor's name and a picture of a bottle of tonic—"or Doc's colleague Emory Bates, the mortician." Dennis pointed to a mug bearing the mortician's name and a picture of a pine coffin.

Sutton raised the mug in his hand. "This here makes me feel like a real solid citizen, Dennis. Though the good

Lord knows there are those in town who'd say my feeling was as wrong as a two-headed calf."

"Why, Luke, you're as solid a citizen as any I know," Dennis declared. "Solider than some if the truth were known,"

Sutton, studying the mug in his hand, frowned.

Seeing his expression, Dennis inquired, "Something wrong, Luke?"

"This here picture." He pointed to the six-gun painted above his name on the surface of the mug.

"It's a gun."

"I can see that. But why—I mean what's it meant to mean?"

Dennis shrugged and glanced at the many mugs in their cubicles on his rack. "Well, Luke, I not only put a man's name on his personal shaving mug but I also put a picture that sort of pinpoints his trade. Like the horse here on Charlie Haines', the liveryman's mug. For you, well, a six-gun seemed to me to be the thing to put on, seeing as how you're known for wearing—and using— one."

A sound that might have been a sigh slid through Sutton's lips. "I reckon you're right, Dennis."

Dennis studied Sutton's strained expression for a moment before remarking, "If it doesn't suit you, Luke—the gun, I mean—I can have another mug made with a picture of—of—" The barber fell silent, apparently at a loss for ideas.

Sutton turned and gazed out the window. Slowly he shook his head. "No, Dennis, there's no need to do that. This mug's fine." He continued staring through the window, seeing nothing but the violent parade of years that lay immediately behind him and the corpses of men who had died because of him. What else could Dennis do, he asked himself. Put a picture of a hammer on the mug he had made up special for me? I'm sure as hell no kind of carpenter. A pair of boots? Neither am I a cobbler. He drew a deep breath. Then, letting it out and turning back to Dennis, he fixed a smile on his face and said, "I do thank you for this." He handed the mug back to Dennis and sat down in a leather chair that faced an ornately gilded mirror.

He squinted at his reflection in the mirror, at the rawboned man squinting back at him. His gunmetal-gray eyes stared steadily at him through narrowed lids. His straight black hair hid his ears from view. His thin lips beneath his narrow nose gave his face a stern expression. His body was leanly muscled, and as he sat there in the barber chair, it seemed ready to spring into hectic action at any moment.

His lips parted in a slight smile. You'll not win any prizes anytime soon for masculine pulchritude, he thought. But then, neither can you be said to be the ugliest man the good Lord ever breathed life into. Why, there's even been a woman or two in your time who went so far as to think you comely.

Cassandra, he thought.

He eagerly conjured her image in the mirror beside him—brown eyes alight, moist lips slightly parted, hair as golden as summer sunlight.

"What have you been up to of late, Luke?" Dennis asked as he stropped a straight razor's blade on the leather strap that hung from the chair in which Sutton sat. "More bounty hunting?"

"Nope. That one bounty hunting trip I made a few months back is just about enough, I reckon, to last me a lifetime."

Dennis applied lather to Sutton's cheeks and chin and then began to scrape it and the stubble it covered away. "What was it you were up to before that? Now, don't tell me. I remember reading all about it in Dan DeQuille's article in the *Territorial Enterprise.*" Dennis frowned, his razor suspended in midair. He stroked his chin. Then, "Indians!"

"Arizona."

"Geronimo, wasn't it?"

"It was."

Dennis shuddered. "Where you got the gumption to go up against those bloodthirsty savages is way beyond me, Luke. I couldn't do it."

"How's your wife, Dennis? The twins?"

Dennis beamed. "They're all three of them fine, Luke. The girls turned five last week and I'm just grateful to God in his heaven that they inherited my Mame's good looks and didn't wind up looking a bit like me."

Dennis talked on then and at length about his beloved wife, Mame, and his twin girls and Sutton, pleased to have successfully steered him away from a discussion of bounty hunting and Indian fighting, listened to the barber's benign tale of domestic bliss.

Later, when he was clean-shaven and his hair had been trimmed and he had paid Dennis for his labors, the barber called out to him as he was leaving the shop. "My Mame told me she saw you walking out with Miss Cassandra Pritchett the other evening, Luke. She told me the love-light she saw burning in Miss Pritchett's eyes was enough to turn the dusk as bright as day. You be careful, Luke, or you'll find out too late that the little lady's gone and put a spoke in your wheel."

Sutton grinned as Dennis guffawed and then he left the barbershop. He made his way through the streets, aware that he was hurrying, his mind on Cassandra Pritchett, almost oblivious to the sudden shrieking of the noon whistle of the Chollar Mine which was followed a split second later by a chorus of other mine whistles. He paid no attention to the thunderous racket resounding from the sun-streaked slopes of Mount Davidson where mines' hoisting works, tall-stacked powerhouses, ore car trestles, and small mountains of waste-rock residue lay baking in the bone-melting heat of the bright July day.

When he reached the International Hotel which had been his destination, he entered it and made his way directly to the dining room where he quickly scanned the room—and saw her.

Cassandra Pritchett was seated alone at a small table by a window. She was wearing a simple day dress of yellow silk which was trimmed with brown braid. It had a front-fastened bodice, stand collar, and fitted sleeves. On her head and framing her face was a brown silk bonnet trimmed with lace and tied beneath her chin with a yellow bow.

Sutton strode across the room. When he reached the table where Cassandra was seated, he sat down across from her, reached out, and took both of her hands in his.

She let out a little cry which caused diners at a near-by table to glance in her direction. Pulling her hands free, she hid them beneath the table and, blushing, glared at Sutton.

"What's wrong?" he asked her, genuinely puzzled at her reaction.

"Sshhh!" she whispered. "People are looking at us."

"You're not glad to see me?"

"Of course I'm glad to see you."

"Then why'd you pull your hands away like mine were on fire or something?"

"Oh, Luke, I do declare you have absolutely no sense of propriety. This is a *public* place."

"You're trying to tell me, I take it, that I should show my affection for you only in some *private* place, is that it?"

"You wouldn't want to create a scandal, would you?"

Sutton's eyes roved appraisingly around the room.

Then, speaking in a somber tone, "After giving the matter at hand my due consideration, I think a little scandal would be just the ticket to liven up this place, which looks more like a morgue to me than a dining room where all these sour-faced folks have come not to eat and enjoy themselves but to mourn."

"It is just that the people here are practicing appropriate decorum and we should endeavor to do the same."

Luke sat up stiffly in his chair. He placed his hands on the table and folded them. He fastened a dour expression on his face.

Cassandra looked at him, looked out the window, looked back at him, began to giggle, clapped a hand over her offending mouth, and then lowered her head to hide the broad smile Sutton's melodramatic imitation of dignity had evoked in her.

"Hush!" he chided her in a pompous voice. "What will the waiters say?"

"Stop it!" she managed to whisper between giggles.

"Stop what, my dear?" he asked in a voice that was a parody of innocence.

"May I be of service?" inquired an obsequious-sounding waiter who appeared at their table.

Sutton abandoned his stern pose and took the menu the waiter handed him. After consulting briefly with Cassandra, he ordered for both of them: broiled filet of sole and tea for her, a rare beefsteak, boiled potatoes, and black coffee for himself.

"I've missed you terribly," Cassandra told him when the waiter had gone.

"How'd you manage to do that?" he asked her in a teasing tone of voice.

She gave him a perplexed stare.

"I mean you and me were together just last night—and right on into early this morning," he reminded her. And then quickly added in a no longer teasing tone, "To tell you the truth, I missed you too."

Cassandra gave him a smile.

"Oh, don't you just love life, Luke? I mean with so many wonderful things to look forward to—like the dance at the Odd Fellows Hall tonight and the Fourth of July picnic tomorrow and, oh, all the good times we shall have together in all the wonderful days after that."

"I'm not much of a man for looking very far into the future. I tend to take things as they come. A day at a time as a rule."

The shadow of a frown passed over Cassandra's face, but when she spoke there remained no trace of it. "But a person must look to the future. Must make plans. One cannot—should not—go through life letting forces outside of oneself control one's destiny."

"You're young, Cassandra. When you're young, you think that all you have to do is flick a finger and the world will jump up and do your bidding. It takes a while before you come to learn that that's not the way things always are."

"Whatever do you mean?"

"Just that this old world of ours has a few tricks up its sleeve and it plays them now and then, and when it does, folks find themselves in hot water they never even suspected was anywheres about."

"You're talking about yourself—your life, aren't you?" Without waiting for Sutton to answer her, Cassandra continued, "The murder of your brother was a terrible thing. But you must put that behind you and go on. Oh, I know that what you said is right. I hate to admit it, but I know that terrible things can happen to people. I try not to think too much about that though. If I did—"

Sutton weighed her words. She was wrong. He knew she was. The murder of his brother, Dan, four years ago was, he was willing to grant, a thing of the past. But it was not something he had forgotten. He knew he would never forget it, despite the fact that he had avenged Dan's death. He considered telling Cassandra that he believed the past never died. That it was like a living thing that shaped a man and made him what he was at any given moment in the present, which in a brief instant would itself become a part of that man's past. But Cassandra's shining eyes and gentle smile deterred him from saying what was on his mind. He did not want to darken her day with his thoughts. It was not his place, he decided, to disillusion her. Life itself, given time, would be enough to do that.

"Spoilsport."

He snapped out of his grim reverie at the sound of the word she had just spoken. "Me? A spoilsport? I reckon you're right. But I'll not be one another minute."

"Promise?"

"I promise."

"Ooohh, doesn't that look delectable?" Cassandra exclaimed as the waiter placed a plate bearing broiled filet of sole garnished with parsley and a slice of lemon in front of her. Then, glancing at Sutton's plate which was buried beneath a bloody beefsteak and boiled potatoes, she asked, "Are you really going to be able to eat all that?"

"I am," he answered. "Got to keep up my strength."

She gave him a concerned look.

"For the dance tonight—and what might come after it," he explained, beginning to grin.

"Shame on you!" Cassandra chastised, but she couldn't keep another smile from illuminating her face.

They had finished their meal and were waiting for the fresh cup of tea Sutton had ordered for Cassandra and the black coffee he had ordered for himself when a man wearing a leather helmet and a bright red shirt appeared in the dining room doorway and shouted Sutton's name, causing heads to turn in mild alarm and a startled someone to drop a fork which clattered onto a plate.

Sutton nodded an acknowledgment of the man's presence. The man beckoned urgently to him. When Sutton didn't move, the man strode across the room, and when he reached the table, said breathlessly, "Luke, it's time!"

"Henry," Luke said, "may I present Miss Cassandra Pritchett? Cassandra, this gentleman's name is Henry Stilling."

"How do, ma'am," Henry said without taking his eyes off Sutton and without seeming to hear Cassandra's "I'm pleased to meet you, Mr. Stilling."

"Come on, Luke, or you'll be late," he persisted.

Sutton raised his cup to his lips and drank from it. Then, "Henry, settle down some. You're acting as edgy as a hen trying to lay a square egg. Miss Pritchett and me, we've not finished our dinner."

"But, Luke—"

"I promise you I'll be along presently, Henry. Tell the boys that, will you?"

"They sent me to fetch you, Luke. I looked all over town. I asked after you in the livery and old Amos over there told me he seen you come in here, so I hightailed it over here—"

"Henry, you did your duty. Now that it's done—go on outside and tell the boys I'll be with them in less than two shakes of a lamb's tail. Will you do that for me, Henry?"

Henry stubbornly stood his ground.

Sutton turned to Cassandra. "Did I tell you the race was set to start at one o'clock sharp?"

"What race?"

"The firemen's hose cart race. I've been picked to join Washoe Engine Company Number Four's team."

"But I thought only firemen were allowed to participate in hose cart races," Cassandra said.

"I'm a fireman," Sutton responded.

"You are?" Cassandra asked, obviously surprised at the news.

"He is, ma'am," Henry stated. "We invited him to join Engine Company Number Four last week after we took a vote on him and not so much as a single black ball showed up against him in the voting."

"Will you stay and watch the race?" Sutton asked Cassandra while simultaneously beckoning to their waiter who hurried up to their table.

"I really should go home," Cassandra replied. "I want to sew a tuck in the dress I'll be wearing to the Firemen's Ball tonight. But I would like to see you race—so, yes, I'll watch."

"Good." Sutton paid the waiter and rose. He escorted Cassandra from the dining room with a hurrying Henry at his heels.

The trio was halfway across the lobby when a woman burst through the front door. When she saw Sutton, she hurried up to him, nervously twisting a pair of lace gloves in her hands.

He halted, as did his two companions, when the woman reached him and said, "I'm sorry to be so brusque, Mr Sutton, but I have to talk to you. I'm sure you're busy but—"

"What did you want to talk to me about?"

"Murder," the woman answered in a bleak voice.

"Luke, it's ten past one," Henry bleated.

"Murder," Sutton repeated thoughtfully, studying the woman who stood before him.

She wore a printed green cotton skirt and a white short gown with full sleeves. Her head was bare and her hands continued to worry the gloves she held in them. Her auburn hair was straight, parted in the middle, and gathered in a small bun at the nape of her neck. Her oval face wore a tense expression and her blue eyes seemed to plead with Sutton.

"I have seen your picture and read about your exploits in the *Territorial Enterprise*, Mr. Sutton," she said in a strained voice. "I never thought I would have need of your services. But now I do very definitely have need of them. I inquired as to your whereabouts and finally learned that you had been seen entering the hotel. So I came here to—"

Sutton said, "Cassandra, if you don't mind, I'd like to have me a talk with—"

"My name is Violet Wilson," the woman volunteered.

Cassandra gave Sutton a cold look and Violet Wilson an even colder one.

"Luke, come on," Henry pleaded.

"Miss Wilson," Sutton said, "I've got some important business to see to. Maybe you and me, we could talk later."

"When?"

"Just as soon as the firemen's hose cart race is over. How'll that suit you?"

Violet was clearly disappointed but she nevertheless nodded her assent to Sutton's suggestion. "I'll wait here in the lobby for you," she told him. "And I do implore you, Mr. Sutton, please don't break our engagement. I am truly desperate and I'm depending upon you."

"She's a very attractive woman, isn't she?" Cassandra remarked as Sutton walked with her toward the door.

"She sure is that."

Cassandra sighed.

"My but you do sound mournful," Sutton observed. "Something's fretting you?"

"It does seem that I have competition for your attentions."

"You don't mean Miss Wilson, do you?"

Cassandra gave Sutton a sidelong glance and arched an eyebrow at him as they left the hotel.

"Miss Wilson sounds like she wants my help not my—what did you call it?"

"Your attentions."

"She's not got anything romantic on her mind if that's what you're driving at."

"You're sure about that?"

Sutton had to admit to himself that he wasn't. "I never saw her before in my life," he told Cassandra as she took his arm and they began walking north. "Besides, you're my best girl. You know you are."

"But not your only girl."

"Now what might you mean by that?"

"Oh, a little bird told me a tale about you—about you and Elsie Spaulding."

"Oh, ho! So you've been spying on me, have you?"

"No, I told you I heard—"

"From a little bird . . ."

"That you walked out with Elsie last week and then you came calling on her two days later."

"But it's you I invited to go to the Firemen's Ball with me, not Elsie Spaulding," Sutton pointed out. Before Cassandra could say anything more, he drew her into the shade of an alley that ran between two stores and gave her a quick kiss.

"Villain!" Cassandra exclaimed as they continued their journey.

"You don't mean that."

She squeezed his arm. "No, I don't. But I do despair of being able to hold on to you, Luke Sutton. You have such an eye for the ladies—and they are not blind to your presence either."

"I—"

"Oh, don't try to deny it. I know it's true. Didn't you chase me in the most shamefaced manner until I succumbed to your manly charms?"

"And glad it is I am that I did and you did."

"Trying to hold on to you is like trying to get a grip on the wind. You're a restless man, Luke. A man who is driven by forces I confess I am at a loss to understand."

"Well, I'll grant you that I'm not a man who's easily hobbled or corralled. I've always had a hankering to see what's over the mountain and up the crick. But don't you fret. I'm not about to run off and leave you in the lurch."

"I most certainly hope not," Cassandra murmured, but her words were lost in the cheers of the throng that greeted Sutton's appearance in front of Knickerbocker Engine Company Number Five's firehouse on D Street north of Union.

Cries of "Better late than never" and "Let the run begin" from the throats of red-shirted and leather-helmeted firemen blended with shouts of "I'm proud to put my money on Young America Company" and "Stand back out of the way" from men in the crowd of onlookers.

"I'll be back once the race is run," Sutton told Cassandra.

"Be careful, Luke," she responded.

"We thought we'd be running the race shorthanded," said one of the members of Washoe Engine Company Number Four's team as Sutton joined them. "Where the hell were you, Luke?"

"I found him in the International Hotel," Henry told the man. "Are we all set, boys?"

The six Washoe men nodded in unison, and as they did so, Henry shouted to a fat man standing on the sidelines that the Washoe team was now ready and eager to compete.

"It's about time," the fat man responded, giving Sutton a glare. He pulled an Ingersoll watch from his pocket, snapped it open, mounted a makeshift platform, and announced, "The hose cart race is finally about to begin, ladies and gents. We have five teams of contestants. Namely, Young America Company, Washoe Company, Knickerbocker, Eagle, and last but by no means least, our neighbor from Gold Hill, the Liberty Engine Company Number One.

"The prize to be claimed by the winner of the race is this." The timekeeper bent down and took the silver loving cup a man in the crowd handed up to him. He held it up for all to see, declaring as he did so, "This cup will be engraved with the name of the winner, ladies and gents, and it will be displayed proudly, I am sure, in the victor's firehouse.

"Now, as official timekeeper for this event, I would welcome the assistance of someone from among you as a second timekeeper to make sure there are no errors in the timing of this race. Who has a reliable watch with a second hand and is willing to assume this important but far from burdensome duty?"

A man in the crowd raised his hand. The timekeeper beckoned to him and both men conferred for a moment, after which the volunteer took his place beside the timekeeper on the platform, his watch in his hand.

"Now then," declared the timekeeper, "the route of the race is as follows. Each team will pull its hose cart from the starting line on D Street to North Street. Upon reaching North Street, the teams will turn west to C Street where they will turn south and race down to Taylor Street. The teams will turn east on Taylor and then north again when

they reach D Street and on to the finish line here in front
of the firehouse. Is that clear, gents?"

The team members cheered.

The timekeeper synchronized his watch with that of his
assistant. He then raised his left hand in the air, and with
his eyes on his own watch, intoned, "Get ready."

Sutton, positioned in the lead on the left side of the hose
cart's wooden tongue with Henry behind him, dug his
boot heels into the dirt, tightened his grip on the four-
wheeled cart's tongue, and got ready.

"Get set," intoned the timekeeper.

Sutton exchanged glances with the two men gripping
the cart's tongue opposite him and with Henry behind
him.

"*Go!*" bellowed the timekeeper at the top of his voice
and brought his left hand down to signal the start of the
race.

The five teams sprang forward, pulling their hose carts,
each of which towered above their heads. The carts' four
huge wheels, which were as tall as the shortest man on the
Washoe team, began to spin, stirring up dust as they did
so.

Beside Sutton ran two of the remaining team members
and two other relief men ran on the opposite side.

Shouts of encouragement from people lining the race
route rang in Sutton's ears as he ran on as fast as he could.
He kept his eyes fixed straight ahead of him as he ran,
blinking and trying to see through the thickening dust
that was being thrown up by the Knickerbocker team's
cart which had veered in front of the one he was helping
to pull.

He and his teammates had just passed the intersection
of D and Mill streets when he yelled to his teammates to
"Pull left!"

One of the two men on his left gave him a puzzled

glance to which he responded, "Knickerbocker's hose is unwinding. It'll trip us up. *Pull left!*"

When the other front man opposite Sutton saw the fire hose beginning to unwind from the drum on Knickerbocker Company's cart, he did as Sutton had ordered, and as a result, the Washoe cart was able to avoid the Knickerbocker's unrolling hose which would have snagged their wheels if they had not changed course in time.

"Not fair," yelled one of Sutton's teammates as they passed the intersection of D and Carson streets. "They've no hose now, so they've less weight to pull."

Sutton redoubled his efforts and shouted encouragement to Henry and his other two teammates to do the same. He sucked great mouthfuls of air into his lungs and with them considerable dust that was swirling everywhere.

They were turning west on North Street when Henry, directly behind Sutton, lost his footing, fell, and was immediately left far behind. One of the two relief men on Sutton's side immediately took Henry's place while the other three, following Sutton's shouted order, got behind the heavy hose cart and began to push it while Sutton and the three men pulling the cart reached C Street and turned south on it.

"I can't make it!" yelled one of the two men on Sutton's left. "Can't get my breath."

"Let go," Sutton ordered, and when the man had obeyed, he then yelled to one of the three men pushing the cart to take over for the winded man.

Behind Sutton's cart raced the Eagle and Young America companies with their carts. On Sutton's right and slightly ahead was Gold Hill's Liberty Company and ahead of both carts by three lengths sped the now hoseless Knickerbocker Company's cart.

As Sutton and his teammates struggled to overtake the

front runner, Liberty Company's cart fell behind and simultaneously as they reached the intersection of C and Taylor streets, Young America Company's cart hit a rut in the road and it overturned, falling against Liberty Company's cart and overturning it so it also went down.

Eagle Company's cart crashed into the wreckage of the other two carts as Sutton yelled at the top of his voice, "It's us or those boys up ahead of us now. Do you want to let those Knickerbockers lick us?"

"No!" yelled his teammates and then two of them began to cough as they choked on the thick dust rising around them.

Knickerbocker Company's cart turned onto D Street and disappeared from sight as Sutton and the others raced down Taylor Street to D Street. As they careened on two wheels onto D Street and then headed north, they were able to see their only remaining competitor far ahead of them and moving fast toward the finish line.

Sutton, his heart hammering against his ribs, gave a rebel yell that was meant to encourage the men on his team, bent forward, and ran on, wind whistling in his ears. The Washoe hose cart hit a rock lying in the rutted road and bounced upward. Slivers from the wooden tongue of the cart ripped through the flesh of Sutton's hands. He cursed the pain he felt and then he cursed the blood that had begun to flow from both of his palms because of the way it was making the cart's tongue slippery and difficult to hold on to.

Shouting encouragement to his teammates, his eyes fastened on the Knickerbocker cart so far ahead of him now, he and the other Washoe men gradually began to narrow the distance between the two carts. By the time they crossed Union Street, Sutton could have reached out and kicked the Knickerbocker cart that was now directly in front of him.

Signaling to the men on his left, he eased the cart to one side and then yelled at the top of his voice, "*Now!*" Working smoothly as a team, the Washoe firemen raced up beside the Knickerbocker cart and then, giving the effort everything they had, they pulled ahead of it to the encouraging shouts of onlookers lining both sides of the street.

Seconds later they approached the finish line—and crossed it. Two of the Washoe men slumped to their knees to lean wearily against the wheels of their hose cart. Sutton, his bloody hands hanging at his sides and his chest heaving, saw the timekeeper consult with his assistant and then announce the Washoe's team company time: "Five minutes and fifty-four seconds."

Almost immediately afterward, the timekeeper cried, "Knickerbocker—five minutes and fifty-nine seconds."

The man behind Sutton who had taken Henry's place happily threw his arms around Sutton and hugged him.

"To the victor go the spoils," declared the timekeeper and beckoned.

"Go ahead, Luke," said one of Sutton's teammates. "Go get it."

Sutton hesitated a moment, but the other men waved him on. He stepped up to the front of the platform on which the timekeeper stood and accepted the silver loving cup the man handed him. He turned, and holding it in both hands, raised it high above his head in triumph. Then, returning to his teammates, he handed the cup to one of them as Henry arrived at the finish line.

"I'm sorry I let you boys down, Luke," he murmured shamefacedly.

Sutton clapped him on the back. "Don't look so down in the dumps, Henry. You did your best."

"But my best wasn't good enough," the disconsolate man lamented.

"Look at it this way, Henry," Sutton said. "You were hell while you lasted."

Henry began to grin.

So did Sutton.

TWO

After seeing Cassandra home, Sutton made his way back to the International Hotel. Along the way he let himself speculate about his upcoming encounter with Violet Wilson.

Murder, she had said, he recalled as he walked along. That's what she wants to talk to me about—murder. I wonder, does she want to talk about somebody who's been murdered or might be murdered? A disquieting thought ambled through his mind. Maybe the lady's got somebody she wants murdered and reckons I might be the man to do the job for her. If that be the case, she's picked the wrong man and I'll waste no time telling her so.

But she didn't look to me to be the kind of lady who was out to hire a man to commit murder for hire. She looked too scared. Far too frightened. But wait up a minute. That could be the very kind of person who'd want to hire somebody to murder somebody else—somebody who is scared stiff of somebody and they've decided the only way to be free of them and their fear is to put that somebody out of commission.

He set his speculations aside, deciding to wait until he had heard whatever Violet Wilson might have to say to him before coming to any conclusions. It was with his step quick and his curiosity aroused that he entered the International Hotel five minutes later. He halted and looked around the lobby. He felt the excitement he had not been fully aware he had been feeling begin to diminish, leaving him feeling faintly frustrated. Because Violet Wilson was not waiting for him in the lobby as she had said she would be at the conclusion of their earlier meeting.

He quickly checked the dining room. She wasn't there.

He went up to the desk clerk and asked, "Did you happen to see the lady I was talking to just before I left here about an hour ago? She had brown hair and sky-blue eyes. She was wearing"—he thought for a moment—"a printed green skirt and a white short gown. She was carrying a pair of lace gloves."

"Yes, sir, Mr. Sutton," responded the desk clerk. "I did see Miss Wilson."

"You know her, do you?"

"I daresay most everyone in town knows Miss Wilson. That would be because of her tireless efforts in raising money to rebuild the city, house the homeless, care for the orphans, and do so many other marvelous things in the awful aftermath of the great fire of 1875 that destroyed so much of our fair city. Not the least of her efforts was her eminently successful attempt at helping citizens to bring suits against their insurance companies when those heartless companies refused to pay in full for the losses so many of us sustained in that terrible time. I'm surprised you don't know Miss Wilson."

"I wasn't living here in seventy-five." Sutton found himself having difficulty in reconciling his impression of Violet Wilson with the valiant fighter and tireless worker the man had just described to him. He had seen a terrified woman. But the desk clerk had spoken of a heroine acting bravely in the face of disaster. His curiosity flared anew concerning Violet Wilson.

"Where might I find her?" he asked the desk clerk.

"You might try her home, Mr. Sutton. Miss Wilson resides at 97 Union Street."

"How long ago did she leave here?"

"It was right after you two had your little chat."

This fellow doesn't miss a trick, Sutton thought.

"I must say she left in rather a hurry. I thought her departure odd at the time."

"Why'd you think it odd?"

"Well, one minute she was sitting there quite calmly"—the desk clerk pointed to a mohair chair—"and the next thing I knew she had leaped to her feet, let out a faint cry, and fled. But not out the front door. No, she turned and made her way into the kitchen, and when I went to see if I could be of any assistance to her—she was quite clearly upset—I learned from our chef that she had run out the back door."

"I'm obliged to you." Sutton left the hotel and when he arrived at 97 Union Street he found himself facing a solidly built frame house which had recently been painted a blinding white except for its shutters, which were a pleasantly contrasting gray. A low post and rail fence surrounded the property which consisted of an oversized lot, the house, and a small outbuilding in the rear. Studying the house, he found himself thinking that it did not look like the lair of a would-be murderess. But, he quickly cautioned himself, just as a man can't tell a book by its cover, neither can he judge a woman by the place where she lived, be it ever so neatly kept and straitlaced-looking.

He went through the gate and up onto the porch. He used the brass knocker to knock on the door. When he received no reply, he knocked again. And again.

The head of a gray-haired woman popped out of the window of a house on the left of the Wilsons' and hung there, adorned with a drooping lace curtain. "She's not to home, Vi's not," the woman called out to Sutton.

"How do you know that?"

"I saw her go out just before one o'clock this afternoon and she's not come back."

"You've been keeping an eye on the place for her, have you?"

"Certainly not. And I don't like what you appear to be thinking. A body can't help but look out the window from time to time and I don't think that's a crime as of yet. Who shall I tell Vi came to call on her?"

Sutton suppressed a smile that was elicited by the busybody's persistence.

"I ought to tell her you came by, whoever you are," the woman declared defensively. "It's the neighborly thing to do. Vi would do the same for me any day."

Sutton doubted it.

"Is it important, the business you have with Vi?"

"Tell her Luke Sutton was here."

Back at the hotel, Sutton arranged for a bath which he took in his room. While sitting and soaping himself in it, he gave some thought to Violet Wilson. Questions sprouted in his mind. What had caused her to cry out and flee the hotel? And why had she chosen to exit through the rear of the hotel instead of the front? Something spooked her for sure, he thought. Else she'd have waited for me to come back here to talk to her. And now—where is she? Maybe she was home when I was at her place, only she wouldn't answer the door for some reason or other.

He shook his head, thinking the busybody next door would have known if she'd returned home. That old biddy don't miss a trick. She probably spends all her waking hours spying on the world from that window of hers.

His thoughts of Violet Wilson gradually gave way to thoughts of Cassandra Pritchett and of the dance they would be attending together in a few hours in the Odd Fellows Hall. He closed his eyes, leaned back in the tub, and let himself luxuriate in the warm water and his pleasant thoughts of holding Cassandra in his arms as they waltzed the whole night through.

That night, Sutton stepped off the elevator and entered the hotel's lobby wearing a black broadcloth frock coat, pearl gray broadcloth trousers, a white ruffled linen shirt with a white paper collar, a black bow-tied silk cravat, black Jefferson shoes, and a gray bowler which matched his trousers.

His dapper appearance turned the head of a young woman who was about to enter the elevator. He touched the brim of his hat to her, causing her to smile and her escort to scowl.

As he strode across the lobby and was about to pass the desk, the night clerk greeted him cheerfully with "Good evening, Mr. Sutton."

"I'm hoping it'll turn out to be one," Sutton responded. "I'd say it's bound to, since I've never yet been to a dance where I didn't have myself a high old time."

"You're attending the dance at the Odd Fellows Hall, I take it?" When Sutton nodded, the night clerk continued, "The dance is, from all I've heard, going to be the social event of the summer season. The Odd Fellows, people tell me, have spared no expense in decorating their hall for the pleasure of the dancers."

"Well, I'd best be on my way. There's a lady waiting on me." Sutton left the lobby and made his way to Cassandra's house where he had to wait twenty minutes for her to get ready.

He decided the wait had been well worth it when Cassandra finally appeared in a ball gown which had a green off-the-shoulder bodice that was edged with frills. It was attached to a blue overskirt which was short in front and which was looped up at the sides and bunched out at the back. She wore a blue velvet band around her neck which was tied at the back in a small bow with its long ends dangling down. Her hair was piled high on her head, had a frizzy fringe in the front, and was decorated with another blue velvet band. On her hands were short evening gloves of green silk and in one of them she carried a fan.

"You're enough to take a man's breath away," Sutton told her as he took her hand, bent down, and brushed it with his lips.

"Flatterer."

Sutton raised his right hand. "It's the truth; I swear it is."

When they arrived at the Odd Fellows Hall, Sutton, with Cassandra holding lightly to his right arm, joined the throng of other couples who were streaming into the brightly lighted hall.

They took their places in the long ticket line, and while they waited their turn to buy tickets to the dance, Cassandra asked Sutton if he had had a pleasant rendezvous.

"Rendezvous?" He gave her a puzzled look.

"With Miss Wilson," she explained.

"I never did see her again," Sutton said, "and if I had, it wouldn't have been at what you could call a rendezvous."

"Then what would it have been? I mean what exactly would you have called it?"

"More like a business meeting."

"Business meeting?"

"You know all about how I've had occasion to go out hunting somebody or other. I told you about how I was paid to go looking for a lady's long-lost brother, to mention one of those kind of things. I reckon Violet Wilson might have something like that on her mind. So any meeting between her and me would be strictly business—at least in my book it would be."

"In your book perhaps. But what about hers?"

"Darlin', I do wish you would just forget all about Violet Wilson. Will you do that for me?"

"I'll try." Cassandra squeezed Sutton's arm. "I'm glad you didn't meet with her. But I'm also curious. Why didn't you?"

"She was gone from the lobby when I got back to the hotel after the race. Hey, here we go!"

Sutton gave the ticket seller a dollar and then gave the tickets he had received to the ticket taker after what seemed another interminable wait. Then he led Cassandra into the hall which was already crowded with people.

She gasped.

He stared.

"Oh, isn't it lovely?" she exclaimed.

"I'd heard they'd worked hard on decorating this place," Sutton said, "but I'd no idea how hard. You're right. It truly is something special."

His eyes roamed about the huge room, examining the carefully laid-out garden walks which were paved with flagstones and lined with real trees in large containers, the flower beds blazing with beauty, and the occasional evergreen tree, all of which had cages where canaries sang hanging from their branches.

"Look over there, Luke!"

Sutton looked in the direction Cassandra was pointing and saw the fountain which was throwing knitting-needle thick streams of water into the air.

Cassandra took him by the hand and led him through the crowd toward the fountain. When they reached it, she cried, "Look, Luke!"

Sutton looked and saw the goldfish swimming in the fountain's basin and the several frogs which were perched on its rim. "It's worth the price of admission just to see how pretty they've made this place," he remarked.

At that moment, the orchestra began to play a Strauss

waltz. Cassandra turned expectantly to Sutton. He took her in his arms.

He stared into her eyes as they glided across the floor among the other dancers and she, with her moist lips slightly parted, met his intense gaze with the faintest of smiles. He was not unaware of the envious looks he received from more than one of the other male dancers nor was he ignorant of the admiring looks those men were giving Cassandra.

They waltzed along garden paths past flower beds and beneath trellised arbors. They circled the fountain, the music made by its splashing water adding to that made by the orchestra and the caged canaries.

When the music stopped, Sutton wrapped his arms around Cassandra and managed to land a light kiss on her left cheek before she, pretending to be scandalized at his impetuousness in such a public place, pushed him away and led him over to the refreshment stand in one corner of the room.

"What'll you have?" he asked her, and when she answered, he filled two crystal cups with punch and handed one to her.

They stood there then, sipping the punch and watching the other dancers, not saying anything except with their eyes as they occasionally exchanged glances.

Later, as they eagerly took part in a lively Virginia reel, Cassandra's face suddenly darkened. A moment later, she withdrew from the dance.

Sutton quickly followed her and asked, "What's wrong?" when he had caught up with her.

"It's that woman," she replied in a harsh tone.

"What woman?"

Cassandra spun around and pointed across the room. Sutton turned and saw Violet Wilson who was standing alone just inside the hall and surveying the room.

"I will say this for her," Cassandra said somewhat peevishly. "She doesn't give up."

The words had hardly been uttered when Violet turned and saw Sutton. Her right hand quickly rose and reached out to him, a gesture that made Sutton think of someone making a silent plea for help. The plaintiveness of her gesture prompted him to say, "I ought to have a talk with her, Cassandra. I—"

"Please don't let me stand in your way. I'm sure I can find some way to amuse myself in the absence of my escort. Perhaps I shall go and watch the goldfish swim in the fountain."

Before Sutton could say anything more, Violet arrived at his side.

"I'm sorry to intrude, Mr. Sutton," she said, her voice strained, "but I simply had to talk to you. I do hope you'll forgive me—that both of you will." She gave Cassandra an apologetic glance.

"This is Miss Cassandra Pritchett," Sutton told Violet. "You and her sort of met earlier today over at the hotel. Cassandra—Miss Wilson."

The women exchanged cool how-do-you-do's, after which Sutton said to Violet, "I came back to the hotel thinking I'd be seeing you, but you were nowhere to be found. So I went on over to where you live, but you weren't to be found there neither. I reckon your next-door neighbor must have told you I'd been by."

Violet shook her head. "No, she didn't. She couldn't actually. You see, I haven't gone back home since I left there a little before one o'clock this afternoon on my way to see you, Mr. Sutton."

"How come you didn't wait at the hotel for me like we agreed you would?" he asked.

Violet looked first one way, then the other, then back at Sutton. "It's so crowded here—so noisy—I wonder, could we go somewhere else to talk? Someplace with more privacy than this where we won't run the risk of being overheard."

"Well, Miss Wilson, as you can plainly see I'm engaged—"

"I know you are and I also know it's rude of me to intrude on you both like this. But I wouldn't have done it if it weren't a matter of the utmost importance. In fact, I had to come just as soon as it seemed safe for me to do so a second time. Please—can we talk?"

Luke turned to Cassandra who, with an airy wave of her hand, dismissed him with the words, "Go ahead, I'm sure I can manage quite well without you," before turning and walking away.

Sutton watched her stop to talk to a group of people and then take the arm of one of the men in the group and begin to dance with him.

"I'm afraid Miss Pritchett is angry with you," Violet murmured. "And it's all my fault."

Sutton, his lips pressed together in a grim line as he watched Cassandra and her new companion whirl about the room, said nothing for a moment. Then, "There's a restaurant about a block from here. We'll go there."

She wanted to come to someplace like this, Sutton thought as he held a chair for Violet, so nobody would hear what she had to say to me. So it must be something—something what? Important? Dangerous? He didn't know, but he did know that he was very much interested in hearing whatever it was Violet wanted to say to him. As he sat down across from her at the table he said, "Now, Miss Wilson, maybe you'll tell me why you didn't wait for me to come back to the hotel to talk to you."

"I couldn't wait because as I was looking out the window I saw Dade Talbot. He was drunk again. I'm sure he saw me, so in order to avoid him, I fled from the hotel by its back door. I didn't dare go home. I thought Dade might come there looking for me. So I went to stay with a friend of mine."

Sutton had no idea what Violet was talking about. Instead of telling her so, he asked, "What is it you wanted to talk to me about, Miss Wilson?"

"It's my fiancé, Mr. Sutton. His name is Aaron Endicott. I want you to try to find him for me. I'm confident that you can. I read in the *Territorial Enterprise* about how you found that young man who had been taken captive as a boy by wild Indians and I also read about your equally successful hunt for Theodore Kimball. So you see I have every reason to believe you will also be successful in your search for Aaron."

A waiter appeared and they ordered coffee and pastries.

"Let's back up a bit for a minute. When we first met over in the hotel today, I asked you what it was you wanted to talk to me about. You said, as near as I can recall, 'murder.' "

Violet nodded.

"Whose murder was it you had in mind?"

"Mine."

Sutton, startled, stared at Violet for a moment, as if he were half expecting her to break into a smile and admit that she was playing a joke on him. When she did neither of those things, he thoughtfully stroked his chin and said, "I'd be obliged to you if you'd explain yourself."

Violet drew a deep breath. "Aaron Endicott and I were —are engaged to be married. We—"

Sutton held up a hand. "You started to say you two *were* engaged to be married. Do you think something's happened to Endicott?"

"Oh, no," Violet exclaimed. "It's just that he's been

gone for nearly a month now and I haven't heard a word from him. I'm sure he's all right, but I confess I have at times begun to have some doubts about our future plans since, as I said, I've had no word from Aaron. As a result, I sometimes think, without even realizing I'm thinking it, that maybe everything really is all over between us, as much as I don't want it to be."

The waiter returned with their coffee and pastries which they both ignored.

"Let's get back to the matter of murder," Sutton said when the waiter had gone. "Who do you think might be going to try to kill you?"

"I don't *think* Dade Talbot is going to try to kill me. I know it. Let me explain. Dade was a suitor of mine before I met Aaron. Actually, he was more of a pest than a suitor. I tried my very best to discourage him, but Dade Talbot is not an easily discouraged man. He persisted in pestering me.

"But then I met Aaron." Violet's eyes became dreamy and her voice softer as she went on. "Aaron and I fell in love at once. I had never believed in that old saw about love at first sight, but I swear to you, Mr. Sutton, that is just what happened to Aaron and me. We really did fall in love at first sight."

Sutton decided to let Violet tell her story in her own way without interruptions. If he had any questions, he would ask them when she had finished.

". . . and once they had a fistfight over me, Dade and Aaron did. As time went on and I continued seeing Aaron, Dade became more and more indignant and importunate, while swearing that he loved me more than life itself."

Sutton noted the embarrassed blush that crimsoned Violet's face.

"He said he could not live without me—without my

love." The flush on Violet's face deepened. "I tried in every way I knew to drive him away, Mr. Sutton, but I failed to do so. He followed me everywhere. He made scenes in public places. He ranted at me and he raved. I began to become truly frightened of him. I tried my best to avoid him, but I was not always able to do so.

"Aaron tried to make Dade stop seeing me. That was what led to the fistfight I mentioned a moment ago. Dade made veiled threats against Aaron which Aaron dismissed as the ravings of a desperate man. I pointed out to him that desperate men were capable of desperate acts. Aaron seemed unconcerned and unafraid. He repeatedly told me not to worry about him, assuring me that he could take care of himself. Aaron was—I mean *is* a brave man, Mr. Sutton

"But when Dade made a threat against my life, Aaron became frightened for the first time—frightened for me and greatly concerned about my safety. You see, Dade had threatened to kill me if Aaron would not abandon me. Dade told me he would see to it, that if he could not have me, neither would Aaron.

"When Dade accosted me on the street the very next day, he was drunk and in a rage. He struck me. The incident alarmed Aaron. It also angered him. He told me he was going to find Dade and kill him. I pleaded with him to calm down and not to do anything so awful. I pointed out to him that he would, by killing Dade, become a murderer subject to hanging if he were found out and apprehended. I finally managed to calm him down.

"But the next day Aaron disappeared. He left behind a note for me." Violet searched through her reticule and came up with a folded piece of paper which she handed to Sutton.

He unfolded it and read:

My darling Vi:

I am going to do something that I may live to regret. But it is something I sincerely feel that, based on the facts as I know them, I must do. I must act to protect you, Vi. I can no longer let myself have a place in your affections if by so doing I endanger your life.

I am therefore going away, so that Talbot will have no reason to want to do you harm. Were I to stay, I fear my resolve would weaken because I would see you from time to time and my deep love for you would make me want to return to you. It is clear to me now that I must go away and never see you again. Be assured, my darling, that I do this with a breaking heart and with eyes blinded by bitter tears. But I do it for you and I hope in time you will find it in your heart to forgive

Your devoted,
Aaron

Sutton folded the piece of paper and returned it to Violet. "I've got a question for you, Miss Wilson."

Violet looked at him expectantly.

"Do you think it's the smart thing to do, sending me out to bird-dog down your fiancé and bring him back here when his being back will no doubt start the pot boiling all over again where Dade Talbot's concerned and maybe put you at risk of getting killed?"

"I love Aaron," Violet answered simply.

"I guess that's about as good an answer as I can expect to get under the circumstances."

"I don't want you to bring Aaron back here, Mr. Sutton," Violet declared. "I don't want you to even tell him that I employed you to find him. I do want you to protect him, keep him safe."

"From?" Sutton prompted, although he thought he knew the answer to his question.

"Dade Talbot. I fear that Dade may, if I continue to resist his advances, do something desperate."

"Like?" Again Sutton was sure he knew the answer to his question.

"Dade is fully aware that I am in love with Aaron. Were he to become desperate enough, he might decide to kill Aaron in the mistaken belief that, with Aaron dead, I might look more favorably upon his suit."

"I'm to be your hired gun."

"I suppose you could put it that way, yes. I want you to protect Aaron—be his bodyguard—secretly, as I said. If and when you do find him, I want you to send word to me. I shall then come at once to wherever he is and he and I will go away to someplace where Dade Talbot will never find us. Mr. Sutton, I am prepared to pay you one thousand dollars for your expert services, more if that is not enough."

"That's enough."

"I'm prepared to pay you half the money now and the other half when you find Aaron. Is that arrangement satisfactory?"

Sutton nodded and Violet withdrew five hundred dollars from her reticule, which she handed to him.

"What can you tell me about Endicott that might help me find him?"

"What sort of things do you want to know?"

As Violet began to speak, the dreaminess returned to her eyes. "Aaron is tall—over six feet tall. He has brown wavy hair and a brown mustache and beard. His eyes are also brown—light brown. He has a sturdy build. Does that help?"

"Some. But lots of men are built sturdy and lots of them have brown hair and eyes and top six feet."

"I have a photograph of Aaron at home."

"Let's go there and I'll take a look at it."

Violet shook her head. "I don't want to go home. In fact, I'm afraid to."

"Because of Talbot?"

"At this juncture, I think I had best remain with my friend until you find Aaron and I can rejoin him and we can go away somewhere."

Once again Violet reached into her reticule. This time she came up with an iron key which she gave to Sutton. "That's the key to my front door. After you go to the house and you've seen Aaron's photograph—it's in a frame on the piano—you can return the key to me at my friend's house."

"Which is where?"

"One fifteen A Street."

"Does Endicott have any family in these parts?"

"No. But he has a sister who lives in Brewster. That's a town north of here."

"I've heard of it. What's this sister's name?"

"Lottie Nevins. Mrs. Harold Nevins. But Lottie won't be able to help you."

"How come you seem so sure about that?"

"Because I wrote to her the very day I received that farewell note from Aaron. Lottie wrote back right away. She said that she had neither seen nor heard from Aaron. She stated that she was as shocked and distressed concerning his disappearance as I was."

"What's her address in Brewster?"

"She lives at number ten Hill Street with her husband."

"What did Endicott do for a living before he disappeared?"

"He was an accountant with the firm of Brent and Faber here in Virginia City."

"What interests did he have other than his job—and you?"

"Well, he liked to play cards—poker mostly but also bridge and cribbage. He loved going for long walks in the outdoors—even in the dead of winter. He read a great deal. I really can't think of anything else."

"Did he have any close friends that you knew about?"

"Aaron had many friends. Everyone liked him. I guess his best friend was a man named Judd Haverstraw. Judd is nearly ten years older than Aaron and I know that Aaron looked up to and admired Judd, although Judd has the reputation of being something of an adventurer if not exactly a rogue."

Violet laughed lightly. "I remember Aaron saying once that he wished he had lived the kind of life that Judd had lived and not the stodgy one he did live. That was the word he used: 'stodgy.' "

"Is there anything else you can tell me about Endicott that might turn out to be helpful to me in my hunt for him?"

Tears appeared in Violet's eyes and her lips began to quiver. "No, nothing except that I love him very much—with all my heart—and want him back ever so badly, Mr. Sutton."

Which, Sutton thought, was not the least bit helpful. "I'll do my best to find him for you, Miss Wilson."

"Oh, I am ever so grateful to you, Mr. Sutton, for being willing to help me in my time of trouble."

"Call me Luke."

"All right, I shall—if you'll call me Violet."

"Well, Violet, I reckon we've gone over all the ground we need to for now."

"When will you start your search for Aaron, Luke?"

"First thing tomorrow. Right after I return your house key to you."

Sutton, after parting from Violet outside the restaurant, returned to the Odd Fellows Hall where he found Cassandra still dancing. Had she been dancing with the same man as when he had left, he would have felt even more jealousy than he did at the moment.

Without hesitation, he strode up to the pair and cut in. Cassandra's partner left her with obvious reluctance as Sutton, hardly missing a beat of the music, began to dance with her.

"Where is she?" Cassandra asked, her face solemn.

"You mean Violet?"

Cassandra's eyes widened and Sutton felt her stiffen in his arms. "So it's not Miss Wilson any longer but Violet. I must say you don't let any grass grow under your feet, Luke Sutton."

"She just now hired me to hunt for her fiancé to whom she's engaged and who she's all set to get hitched to, if and when I can find the fellow for her. So there's no need for you to be jealous of her."

"Me? Jealous of her?" Cassandra assumed a disinterested air.

"To tell you the truth though," Sutton whispered in her ear, "your being jealous makes me feel real good. I'd feel as bad as a buck with a broken leg if you didn't give a hoot in the holler about whether I ran off from you to chase after some other woman."

"I wouldn't put such behavior past you."

"Nor would I ever expect you to turn into a wall-flower when I was gone—which, it was plain to see, you didn't do tonight."

"What was I supposed to do? Simply sit and await your return instead of trying to enjoy myself?" Cassandra's eyes flashed fire as she stared at Sutton.

He shook his head. "Nope. I'd never expect the prettiest girl at the party to do anything like that."

The fire faded fast from Cassandra's eyes and was replaced by the kind of dreaminess Sutton had seen in Violet's eyes when she had spoken to him of Aaron Endicott.

"When do you plan to go looking for Miss Wilson's intended?"

"First thing tomorrow."

"Oh, Luke!"

"What's wrong?"

"The Fourth of July picnic is tomorrow afternoon."

"I know and I know too that I intended to take you to it. But I've got to be about running down Aaron Endicott, on account of till I do, Violet's life is in danger." He told Cassandra what Violet had told him.

"I understand," she said when he had finished doing so. "I do hope you'll find Mr. Endicott and that no harm will come to Miss Wilson in the meantime from that awful Mr. Talbot."

"I promise I'll make up the missed picnic to you once I get back from wherever it is I'm going."

"Be warned, Luke. I shall most definitely hold you to that promise."

"I might even come up with a way to make good on my promise that'll turn out to be a whole lot more exciting for the two of us than a Fourth of July picnic could ever turn out to be," Sutton remarked, giving Cassandra a wicked wink.

She eagerly tightened her hold on him as they continued dancing as close to each other as they could possibly get.

THREE

Early the next morning Sutton, his mind full of happy thoughts of the time he had spent with Cassandra the night before, walked whistling up to Violet Wilson's front door. He unlocked it with the key she had given him and stepped inside.

He found himself in a dim parlor which spread out on both sides of the door. By a window at one end of the room was a piano and on the piano was the photograph he had come to see. He went over to the piano and picked up the gilt-framed photograph.

So this is Aaron Endicott he thought as he stared at the man who stared right back at him.

The photograph showed Sutton a smiling man who had a broad forehead and slightly arched eyebrows which gave him a faintly mischievous look. Despite the man's smile, there was something about his eyes which gave him a look of determination. His cheeks and chin were covered by the beard Violet had mentioned. His lips were full, the upper one half hidden by the mustache she had also mentioned. His nose was slightly oversized with two nostrils that flared up and outward like the wings of a small V.

He's not such a bad-looking fellow Sutton thought. No wonder Violet Wilson turns all moonstruck and calf-eyed when she starts talking about him. He looks to me—his eyes do and the set of his lips—like a man who could turn out to be stubborn. The kind of jasper polite Christian

folks would call strong-willed. The kind of jasper who
could, if the need arose, do things he'd rather not have to
do. Like go off somewhere and leave the love of his life
pining behind him.

Go off where?

Sutton, the question echoing faintly in his mind, set the
photograph back on the piano. As he did so, he heard the
front door open behind him. He turned quickly, automati-
cally reaching for the gun he was not wearing, as was his
habit when in town.

A man lurched into the room and stood there, one hand
clutching the doorknob, the other pawing the air in front
of him as if he were seeking to grasp something elusive.
"Where is she?" he roared.

"Who might you be looking for?" Sutton inquired
mildly, almost certain he was confronting Dade Talbot
whom Violet had told him about and completely certain
that the man, whoever he was, was drunk.

"She's here. I know she is." The man let go of the doorknob and lurched a few steps farther into the room. "Vi,
it's me, Dade," he called out. "Where are you?"

"Miss Wilson's not here," Sutton told Talbot.

Talbot turned and stared bleary-eyed at him for a moment before barking, "Who the hell are you?"

"I happen to be a friend of Miss Wilson's. Name's Luke
Sutton."

"Well, *I* happen to be her fiancé and as such I want you
to march right on out of here, Mister Friend-of-Miss Wilson's."

Sutton didn't move.

"March, Sutton!" Talbot ordered and pointed to the
open front door.

"I'm taking no orders from you, Talbot."

Talbot's eyes narrowed. "I don't know you from Adam.
How come you know my name?"

"Miss Wilson told me all about you. She told me about how you've been chasing after her when she's made it plain as day to you that she don't want nothing more to do with you. She told me you hit her. Well, now that we've met, *I* want to tell you, should you ever take a misguided notion to do a dastardly thing like that again, you'll have me to reckon with."

Talbot spluttered wordlessly as he continued to glare at Sutton, his huge hands flexing at his sides. He was not a tall man but he was heavier than Sutton. His shoulders were thick; so was his waist. His chest was nearly as big as a barrel. His square head jutted forward in a pugnacious manner which had the effect of hiding most of his neck, making it seem to anyone facing him that the man's head rested on his broad shoulders. His thick black eyebrows matched the color of his curly hair. His nose was bent out of shape; it seemed to twist down toward his thick lips and sharply pointed chin.

"Vi!" he yelled at the top of his voice.

"I told you before, Talbot. She's not here."

Talbot snarled something unintelligible and then went weaving out of the living room. Sutton heard him climbing stairs and then he heard the sounds the man made as he moved from room to room on the second floor.

Minutes later, after returning to the first floor and searching its rear rooms, Talbot reappeared in the living room. "Where the hell have you got her?"

"I've not got her nowhere," Sutton replied placidly.

"Are you after her too? If you are, be warned. I already ran off one fellow who had his eye on her and I'm up to running you off too."

"Get out," Sutton ordered. "You've got no business here. You're trespassing."

"Oh, it's trespassing I am, is it? What about you? I suppose you've got every right in the world to be here in the absence of the rightful owner of this house by which I mean Violet Wilson."

"I'm here at her request. I already told you that. Now, listen up, Talbot. I'm going to tell you one more time to get out. If you don't—I'll get you out. You got that?"

Talbot smirked and in a mocking voice repeated what Sutton had just said. Then he lunged forward and his hands closed around Sutton's throat.

Sutton tore at Talbot's hands but it was several minutes, which seemed to him like an hour, before he was able to break the man's grip on his neck and send him staggering backward with a well-aimed blow to the gut.

Talbot struck a table that stood against a wall, almost overturning it. An empty vase fell from it to the floor and broke at his feet. Muttering deep in his throat, Talbot lunged again.

This time Sutton was ready for him. Sidestepping deftly, he let Talbot go surging harmlessly past him. Then, turning swiftly on his heels, he went after his attacker and seized him firmly by the collar and the seat of the pants. Half carrying and half dragging him, he got Talbot to the open front door through which he unceremoniously threw him.

As Talbot went flying from the porch to land face down on the front lawn, Sutton stepped out onto the porch and locked the front door. He was starting down the steps when he saw the horrified face of the woman next door framed in her open window. He solemnly touched the brim of his hat to her and stepped around the downed Talbot who managed to raise himself up partway and let out a roar of impotent rage. As Talbot slowly sank back down to the ground, a victim of both the spirits he had consumed and Sutton's blunt handling of him, he managed to shout, "I'll get you for this, Sutton, you high-handed sonofabitch!"

Sutton ignored him as he set out for number one fifteen A Street, the home of Violet's friend with whom she had said she was staying temporarily in an effort to avoid Talbot.

When he reached his destination, his knock on the door was answered by a pert young woman who, in response to his question, told him that, yes, Violet Wilson was there and she supposed he was Luke Sutton, the man Vi had told her so much about.

"Yes, ma'am, that's me," he said as she introduced herself as Adele Fenton and then led him to the kitchen where he found Violet Wilson seated at a table peeling potatoes.

"Oh, it's you, Luke," she cried when she saw him. She dropped what she was doing and got to her feet.

"Here's your key, Violet." He handed it to her. "I had company while I was at your house this morning."

"Company?"

"If you'll excuse me," Miss Fenton said and started to leave the room.

"I'd like you to stay and hear what I've got to say," Sutton told her. "It may turn out to be of concern to you as well as to Violet."

"You sound positively ominous, Luke," Violet ventured uneasily. "What happened?"

"Dade Talbot happened," he answered. "He showed up at your place just as I was fixing to leave. He was looking for you. I told him to stay away from you, but I doubt he took my advice to heart. I got rid of him, but I reckon he'll keep on trying to find you. Should he ever happen to show up here, I'd say you ladies ought to send for the police the minute he does and have him locked up on charges of how he's been harassing you."

"We'll do just that, Mr. Sutton," Miss Fenton assured

him. "This business has gone far enough—too far in my humble opinion."

"I'll be on my way now," Sutton said and started for the front door.

Violet, hurrying after him, said, "I want to thank you again for being willing to assist me, Luke. I want you to know how much I do appreciate your help. And there's one other thing I'd like to say to you."

Sutton stopped at the front door. "What's the other one thing?"

"Be careful."

"Violet, there've been those who've known me who claimed I didn't have as much brains as God gave geese. So I make it my business to be careful in case those folks should turn out to be right." He gave her a grin.

"Goodbye, Luke."

"If I find Endicott for you, I'll send word to you here at Miss Fenton's."

Sutton went directly to the offices of the accounting firm of Brent and Faber where he asked a young man seated behind a desk just inside the entrance if he could speak to someone about Aaron Endicott.

"Mr. Endicott is no longer with us, sir," the clerk informed Sutton. "He has not been associated with our firm for over a month."

"You must have misunderstood my question," Sutton said.

"Sir?"

"I didn't ask to speak to Endicott. I know he's not here. I asked to speak to someone *about* him."

"Oh." The clerk ran nervous fingers through his hair. "Well, you could speak to the firm's senior partner, Mr. Simpson. Shall I make an appointment for you to see him at some mutually convenient time?"

Sutton leaned over the clerk's desk. "I'm a busy man. So, I reckon, is this Mr. Simpson of yours. Now two busy men like Simpson and me, we ought to get right down to the dirt on something as important as the business I have with him. So suppose you just point me the way to him."

The clerk, taken aback by Sutton's faintly menacing stance and tone, rose quickly from his chair and backed up several steps. "I'll tell Mr. Simpson you're here Mr.— Mr.—"

"Sutton."

The clerk vanished down a dim hall and then reappeared a few minutes later to announce, "Mr. Simpson will see you now, Mr. Sutton. Right this way."

The clerk led Sutton to an office at the end of the hall into which he was obsequiously ushered.

"Mr. Sutton, I presume?" said a rotund man standing with his hands clasped behind his back in front of a large open window. I'm Charles Simpson. What can I do for you?"

"I've been hired to find Aaron Endicott, Mr. Simpson. I thought I ought to come by here and have a talk with you about him and how he up and disappeared so sudden. Find out anything you could tell me that might help me track him down."

"Endicott didn't disappear, Mr. Sutton."

Sutton's eyebrows arched. "He didn't?"

"Disappeared implies a sudden action, I rather think. But Endicott spent several days here at work putting his business affairs in order before he actually left. He arranged to transfer his work to other accountants in the firm—that sort of thing. He was a very methodical, not to mention reliable, employee."

"He didn't tell you where he was going?"

"No, he didn't nor did he tell anyone else in the firm either. Which is unfortunate, since we are holding a rather substantial paycheck in the amount of one hundred and seven dollars that is due him. We have no idea how to get it to him, since we are unaware of his present whereabouts.

"Mr. Sutton," Simpson said after a pause, "I'm curious about something. May I ask who hired you to try to find Endicott?"

"Miss Violet Wilson did."

"Ah, yes, the lovely Miss Wilson." Simpson clucked his tongue and sorrowfully shook his head. "A shame that Endicott's alliance with Miss Wilson didn't work out. He didn't tell anyone here why he was leaving the firm, but I couldn't help suspecting that his relationship with Miss Wilson had turned sour."

"How long did Endicott work for you?"

"Over three years. And I must say he was a most dependable employee and an absolutely splendid accountant. He almost never made a mistake. He seldom missed a day of work, and when he did, it was for the very best of reasons. We were truly sorry to lose him."

"Where did he go on his vacations, do you know?"

"Yes, I do know as a matter of fact. He and Miss Wilson made two trips that I know of into the Sierra Nevada mountains where, Endicott gave me to understand, they lived a rather Spartan outdoor life. Endicott was apparently something of a nature lover. I suppose that manner of living was something of a counterbalance to his more settled and routine existence in a city the size of ours and in a profession that offers little in the way of excitement to an adventurous young man such as Endicott was in his spare time."

"I thank you for your time, Mr. Simpson."

"If you should happen to locate Endicott, tell him for me, Mr. Sutton, that we miss him and want him back at his desk if he will consider returning to us."

"I'll be sure to do that."

Sutton returned to the hotel where he changed his clothes and then paid a month's room rent in advance.

When he left the hotel later that morning, he was wearing a black flat-topped Stetson, a tan bandanna, a brown bib shirt, black low-heeled army boots into which the legs of his worn and faded dungarees were tucked. And a gun.

The gun was a six-shot Remington Improved Army Revolver, Model 1875, caliber .45. Its barrel measured seven-and-a-half inches. Sutton had removed the lanyard ring that had been in its butt when he bought it, so it would draw easily. For the same reason, he had spent hours carefully smoothing and honing the action until it met his strict standards for a weapon meant to be able to save his life or end the life of an enemy.

The gun hung in the black leather holster of a cartridge belt strapped around his lean waist. He had carefully oiled the holster to make drawing the gun as easy as possible and he had made certain that every loop in the belt contained a shell.

He made his way to the livery where he was greeted cheerfully by the stableman.

"Haven't seen you in nigh onto a whole week, Luke. Thought maybe you'd given up riding a horse and looking at the world from between its ears."

"I don't know how you can say such a thing to a man like me, Simon, who was riding a horse, thanks to my pa, before I'd learned how to walk."

Simon smiled. "Your dun's in fine condition, Luke. I've grained him good like you ordered. Rubbed him down once a day. Had my boy exercise him every day too. His shoes are sound and your gear—my boy worked goose grease into the leather. You'll find everything in apple-pie order."

"I'm obliged to you, Simon, I truly am. It's a comfort to

know I can leave my mount with somebody who prizes horseflesh the way you do. How much do I owe you this time around?"

When Sutton had settled his boarding bill, Simon said, "I know it's none of my business, Luke, but I wonder where you're headed. On another hunting expedition?"

"You hit the nail on the head, Simon."

"Who are you after this time?"

"Fellow name of Aaron Endicott."

"You don't mean that accountant fellow, do you? The one who's been courting Violet Wilson?"

"That's the one."

"But he's no desperado."

"I know that. I don't only go out after desperadoes, Simon. Sometimes I go out after lovelorn strays like Endicott."

"Lovelorn is he? Well, I'm not the least bit surprised to hear that. Violet Wilson is just as pretty as a new-born summer day."

Sutton made his way to the stall in which his dun was quartered and proceeded to get the animal ready to ride. He noticed that his saddle blanket had been washed, for which he was grateful. He noticed too that his saddle leathers were soft and supple as a result of the goose grease the stableman's boy had worked into them.

Minutes later, he led his dun out of the livery, said goodbye to Simon, and rode out of town heading north.

The following afternoon Sutton reached the town of Brewster which lay sprawled in an apparently unplanned fashion between the broken foothills of the southernmost tips of the Humboldt and Trinity ranges.

The rumbling of his stomach made him halt in front of the first restaurant he came to. He dismounted and tethered his dun to a hitchrail.

Once seated at a table with his back to the wall inside the restaurant, he ordered a steak, baked potato, buttered bread, and black coffee. When the steak came, he told the white-aproned waiter that, since it looked to him to be the runt of the litter, he'd have two. His second steak arrived minutes after he had finished his first and it was not until he had consumed that one that his stomach, finally appeased, at last fell silent. He forked the last of his potato into his mouth, and then, after sopping up the juices the two steaks had left on his plate with a piece of bread, he ate the bread, washing it down with the last of the coffee in his cup.

"More coffee?" inquired his waiter who appeared at his elbow with a coffee pot in his hand.

"I'd appreciate it." As the waiter refilled his cup, Sutton said, "I'm here to visit friends of mine. Their names are Harold and Lottie Nevins. They live at number ten Hill Street. Do you know where that's at?"

"That's up on the ledge. That's what we call it—the ledge. It's over on the west side of town. It's a kind of plateau that's higher up than the rest of Brewster. Their house is on the east end. It's got a real rundown look about it. Ask anybody. They'll point out the Nevins place to you."

When Sutton arrived at the Nevins place, he halloed the house and a worn-looking woman came outside through the front door which leaned to one side on its rotting leather hinges.

"My name's Luke Sutton, ma'am. I've come to have a talk with you if you happen to be Lottie Nevins."

"That's me," the woman said in a weary voice. She pushed strands of prematurely graying hair away from her face, her narrowed eyes on Sutton. "I don't know you."

"No, ma'am, you don't. But we've got us a mutual acquaintance. Her name's Violet Wilson."

The woman took a step backward, one hand reaching blindly for the wooden door.

"Now don't you go and run off on me, Miz Nevins. I come a long way to talk to you."

"It's about Aaron, isn't it? You want to talk about Aaron." Without waiting for Sutton's nod that came in response to her words, she hurried on, "I don't know anything about him, so there's nothing to talk about. Go away."

As Mrs. Nevins turned sharply and started to step inside her house that was little more than a hovel, Sutton dismounted and seized her by the right wrist. "I don't usually step down from the saddle less I'm asked to, but like I said before, I come a long way to talk to you and I don't want you to turn me away before we can have ourselves that talk. I don't mean your brother no harm, ma'am. I can assure you of that. I hope you'll believe me. Violet Wilson hired me to find him on account of she loves your brother a whole lot and is pining away without him. I thought you might have seen him. I thought maybe you could tell me where he might be. If you can, I'll go to him and then send word to Miss Wilson who'll come and join up with him again and then the two of them plan to go away somewhere together. She told me she wrote you about the trouble that made your brother hightail it out of Virginia City for parts unknown."

"Yes, Violet wrote to me asking about Aaron. I wrote back that I didn't know a thing about where he was or might be."

Sutton released his hold on Mrs. Nevins' wrist. The woman saddened him. She had not struggled or tried to free herself from him. She seemed to have given in to him without a fight. To life as well, he suspected. Defeat was evident in the harsh lines on her prematurely aged face and in her gaunt and slightly stooped body.

"When a fellow like your brother looks for a place to go to ground, chances are he'll go where his kin are at. That's why I come here, Mrs. Nevins. I think Endicott might be here."

"He's not. He never was."

"You'd be doing him and Miss Wilson a big favor if you could help me track your brother down. They love each other a lot. They ought to have their chance to live full and happy lives together. So I'll ask you this. Where do you think your brother might be?"

"New York City," Mrs. Nevins answered dully.

"New York City," Sutton repeated. "That's a far piece from here. What makes you think he'd head there?"

"He always wanted to go there ever since he read about all the things—shows and stuff—they got back there. He and Vi planned to move there after they married."

Violet never told me any such thing, he thought. "New York City, huh? If your brother's there, it's safe to say I never will find him."

Sutton noted the look of relief that briefly flooded Mrs. Nevins' face. "Is your husband to home, ma'am?"

She shook her head.

"I'd like to have a chance to talk to him too. He might be able to tell me something helpful about your brother that you can't." Or won't, he thought.

"Harry's down in town."

"Whereabouts?"

"How should I know?"

Sutton subtly shifted position so that he could see through the front door. He saw no sign of Harold Nevins. "I'm obliged to you, ma'am. I reckon it's time I was moseying on." Sutton touched the brim of his hat to Mrs. Nevins and climbed back into the saddle. As he rode down the slope leading from the ledge, he heard Mrs. Nevins slam the door of her house behind him.

He drew rein when he reached a grove of quaking aspens and moved the dun in among them. He dismounted, and leaving his horse to browse with its reins trailing, he hunkered down with his arms crossed on his knees, his eyes on the Nevins house up above him.

He was still there, his eyes still on the Nevins house when the sun started down toward the horizon, the birds singing in the aspens' branches and the occasional *clack* of his dun's teeth as it browsed the only sounds in the vicinity.

The sun had grown orange and then red and had nearly reached the horizon when he heard a sound that was made by no bird or horse. Instantly, he was on his feet with his gun drawn and turning in the direction from which the sound—a footfall he was sure—had come. He stood his ground as the sound was repeated several times. Whoever it is that's coming this way, he thought, don't care who hears him.

A man lumbered clumsily into sight. He halted when he saw Sutton, his eyes dropping to the gun held steady in Sutton's hand.

"Who the hell are you and what are you doing skulking around out here in the woods?" barked the red-eyed and unarmed man.

"I'll ask you the same question," Sutton responded, holstering his forty-five.

"I'm Harry Nevins," was the man's answer. "That's my house up there on the ledge."

"That's where you live with your wife, Lottie, and her brother, Aaron, I've been told."

"Whoever told you that's a liar," Nevins muttered. "It's just me and Lottie living up there all by our lonesome."

Sutton tried to ignore the disappointment he was feeling as a result of the failure of his attempt to trick Nevins.

Nevins pulled a pint bottle from his hip pocket and raised it to his lips. He consumed the little whiskey that remained in the bottle and then, holding it out in front of him, he let it fall to shatter on a rock by his boots.

"Where is Endicott if he's not to home?"

Nevins tore his eyes away from the shards of his broken whiskey bottle and gave Sutton a suspicious look.

"What business is it of yours where my brother-in-law is or isn't?"

Without waiting for an answer or even seeming to expect one, Nevins turned his attention again to his shattered whiskey bottle. "Damnation!" he snarled. "I spent my last dime for that bottle and I'll sure enough and sad to say have me one helluva thirst by the time I can buy me the next one."

Sutton, thinking he saw a chance to get any information Nevins might possess, thrust a hand into his pocket and came up with a gold eagle. He held the coin up, so that it caught the last light of the sun. Nevins stared mesmerized at it for a moment and then at Sutton who said, "I'm looking for your brother-in-law, Nevins. If you can help me find him, this money's yours."

"He works in Virginia City," Nevins said, his eyes returning to the gold coin in Sutton's hand.

"Not anymore he don't," Sutton countered. "He skipped town. Seems he had a problem with his fiancé and another gentleman who had an eye on his lady."

Without taking his eyes from the eagle, Nevins said, "You know about that, do you?"

"I don't mean Endicott any harm," Sutton assured him. "I've been hired by Miss Violet Wilson to find him, so she can come to wherever it is he's at and the two of them can pick up where they left off before he left town."

"How do I know you're telling me the truth?"

"You don't. But I am." When Sutton twisted his fingers, the gold coin glittered.

Nevins licked his lips. "He was here."

"I talked to your wife. She said he wasn't."

"Well, she lied. Aaron told us not to tell nobody he'd been here."

"So that's why your wife wrote to Miss Wilson and claimed she'd not seen Endicott."

Nevins shook his head. "Lottie told the truth when she answered the Wilson woman's letter. Aaron hadn't been by here at that point. He come by later."

"Is he up at the house now?"

"You ought to pay more than ten dollars for what I can tell you about Aaron," Nevins said, giving Sutton a sly look. "What about twenty?"

Sutton nodded.

Nevins said, "He's gone. He was only with us two days. Then he left as sudden as he came."

"Where did he go?"

"He didn't say. Wouldn't tell us. Just said he had to go find a job before he ran out of spending money, which he let on he was right on the verge of doing. Lottie, she begged him to say where he was going. Wanted to keep in touch with her only brother she told him. She told him she'd heard of how folk lost track of one another when one of 'em went wandering like it appeared Aaron meant to do. But he was stubborn as a Missouri mule. Wouldn't let on as to where he was headed, even though Lottie, she cried and carried on about losing her baby brother forever and ever."

"When exactly did he leave your place?"

"The day before yesterday."

"Was he mounted or on foot?"

"He had him a horse."

"What kind of horse—what color?"

"A sorrel."

"Which way did he go when he left?"

"West. Due west." Nevins took a step toward Sutton. "That's all I can tell you." He held out his right hand.

Sutton paid him the agreed-upon twenty dollars for the information he had provided and then he went to his horse and swung into the saddle.

As Sutton rode out of the grove, heading due west, Nevins began to retrace his steps, heading back toward Brewster, and Sutton supposed, the nearest saloon which would soon, he was sure, relieve the man of the twenty dollars he now had in his pocket.

FOUR

At the edge of town, after having bought some provisions which he stored in his saddlebags, he drew rein and proceeded to ask passers-by if they had seen a brown-bearded man riding a sorrel head out of town two days earlier. The fifth man he asked answered, "Sure, I did. You must mean Aaron Endicott."

"That's the man. You know him, I take it?"

"I peddle butter and eggs in town. Took some up to the Nevinses a few days ago and Harry introduced me to Endicott. Said the man was his brother-in-law."

"Did you by any chance have a word or two with Endicott two days back when you spotted him heading out of town?"

"I did. Affable gent, Aaron was. Friendly as a petted pup."

"Did he say where he was headed?"

The man thought for a moment and then, "No, not as I recollect."

"What did he say?" Sutton prodded.

"Well, he said he was headed west to look for a job. I said that sort of surprised me, because Lottie Nevins had told me a while back that her younger brother was some sort of big shot down in Virginia City. Aaron said he was never no big shot anyplace, and besides, he'd left Virginia City to do some traveling."

"Anything else you remember about what he said?"

"That was just about it. We only talked for maybe a minute or so before he rode on out."

"I'm obliged to you."

Sutton rode until the land around him was drowned in purple shadows. Then he made camp for the night at a spot he had chosen because it had plenty of both water and wood. He watered both himself and his horse at a shallow stream and then broke off part of a deadfall which he used to build a fire.

He took a can of tomatoes and a loaf of bread from his saddlebag, items he had bought before leaving Brewster, and opened the can with a bowie knife he took from his boot. Sitting cross-legged in front of his fire, he ate part of the loaf of bread and all of the tomatoes.

After finishing his meal, he stripped and hobbled his dun, spread his ground tarp, which he covered with his blanket, and placed his saddle at the head of the bed he had made. He pulled off his boots and lay down on his blanket, tilting his Stetson over his eyes and placing his six-gun beside him, his head pillowed on his saddle.

He folded his arms across his chest. He turned on his right side. Minutes later, he turned over on his left side. Sleep escaped him. He took off his hat, set it aside, and stared into the low flames of the dying fire. They sent their orange light flashing into the surrounding darkness, vanquishing it only briefly.

He thought about Aaron Endicott, what little he had been able to learn about the man. Endicott liked the outdoors according to Violet. Simpson, Endicott's employer, had said that Endicott and Violet had spent his last two vacations camping out. He knew what Endicott looked like. He knew he was riding a sorrel. He knew that Endicott was headed west and he seemed, according to the man Sutton had last spoken to, to have no intention of returning to Virginia City. Endicott, according to that man, intended to find himself a job somewhere.

Sutton's thoughts shifted. He found himself thinking of Violet Wilson, of the woman's loveliness. He found himself envying Endicott—at least the Endicott who had lived in Virginia City before Dade Talbot had torn apart both his and Violet Wilson's lives.

His thoughts shifted again and he found himself remembering what he knew he could never forget—the way his own life had been so violently disrupted and changed forever four years ago. In the flames of the fire danced the smiling face of his younger brother, Dan. His body stiffened as he saw the boy being murdered. And then he saw himself following the many devious trails that had led him at last to his prey—the four men who had killed Dan and almost killed him as well.

He felt a certain sympathy with Endicott because, he realized, they shared a similar ugly experience. Both of them had been uprooted from the lives they had been living by the unwanted intervention of others. He knew how hard that could be to endure. But, he thought, at least Endicott hasn't lost the person he loves the way I lost Dan.

Not yet.

He wondered where the words and the thought they embodied had come from. And then he knew. Dade Talbot, he was convinced from his brief but brutal encounter with the man and from what Violet had told him, was capable of violence. That violence could still turn out to be directed against Violet, he felt sure, and in his certainty, he began to wonder if he had done the right thing by leaving her unprotected and virtually alone back in Virginia City in the face of the potential danger that Talbot posed to her. Maybe he should have brought her with him on his search for her fiancé. No. She would only have slowed him down. He would have had to constantly be looking out for her well-being, and in so doing, he surely would be hobbled in his hunt for Endicott.

He decided he had done the right thing, but still his uneasy thoughts persisted and successfully kept at bay for nearly two hours the sleep he sought.

He awoke before dawn, sat up, shook out his boots, and then pulled them on. He holstered his gun, clapped his hat on his head, got up, and made his way, carrying his blanket and tarp, through the thick fog that had settled on the land where his horse stood as still as a stone statue.

It nickered as he approached it. Its skin rippled as he ran a hand over its body that was damp from the fog. He had his gear on the animal a few minutes later and a few minutes after that he had his bedroll in place. After filling his canteen at the stream, he rode out under a sky filled with stars as yet undimmed by any sign of the sun.

Later, as the sky began to lighten, Sutton spotted a large patch of tall-stemmed evening primrose. Their yellow night-blooming flowers were only now beginning to close and the hordes of night-flying moths that surrounded them were beginning to disperse. He rode up to them, got out of the saddle, and pulled up some of the plants by their roots, choosing those which bore no flowers, indicating that they were less than two years old and had roots that had not yet turned bitter.

Since there was no water in the vicinity, and since he did not want to wait to eat the roots he broke from the plants because of his intense hunger that was growing stronger with each passing minute, Sutton rubbed as much of the dirt from the roots as he could on a thick patch of grass. He climbed back atop the dun and moved out, chewing on the primrose roots as he went. He pocketed those that remained when his hunger was appeased.

As the sun rose, he urged the dun into a gallop in an

effort to narrow the distance between himself and his quarry who had a two-day head start on him. When the sun was high, he stopped to let the dun graze some grass that was sprinkled with sweet clover while he sat in the shade afforded by the animal's big body and took from his pocket and ate the last of the evening primrose roots.

Less than an hour later, he was headed west again. To escape the intense heat of mid-afternoon, he drew rein and dismounted. He led his horse under a rocky overhang where he stripped it and rubbed it down with handsful of wheat grass that was growing nearby. Later, when the sun was almost down and some of the day's heat had begun to dissipate, he continued his journey. His eyes roamed the surrounding countryside as he searched for any sign of Endicott. He found none that evening nor did he find any the following morning as he neared the majestic mountains of the Sierra Nevada range, the snow-topped peaks of which glistened in the bright sun. His eyes narrowed as he spotted the thin sliver of smoke rising in the distance on his left which was almost invisible against the dark bulk of the mountains looming beyond it.

Campfire, he thought. Built either by somebody who don't care if he's seen or don't know how easy smoke can be spotted by anybody with even half an eye. He turned his dun and rode at a trot toward the smoke, his eyes on the ground ahead of him. He came upon sign left by a rider when he was a little more than halfway to his destination. He slowed the dun to get a better look at the ground. Lame, he thought as he studied the four hoofprints, three of which dug deep into the soft ground. The fourth, made by the horse's right rear leg, was indistinct. The horse that left this sign's crippled, he thought. It's favoring it's right rear leg.

He got back into the saddle, and with his right hand on the butt of his Remington, he cautiously approached the campfire. He was still a half mile from it when he saw that it had been abandoned by whomever had been riding the horse—the sorrel horse—that now stood forlornly beside the fire that was little more than hot ashes.

When he reached the spot, Sutton dismounted and went up to the sorrel that had no saddle or bridle. He noted the way the animal's right rear hoof was twisted, so that its front end lay limply against the ground because the horse would not or could not put any weight on it.

He glanced at the dying fire. Whoever belongs to that horse was here no more than an hour ago, he thought. Was it Endicott? He couldn't be sure. The world's chock-full of sorrel horses, he thought. He looked back at the horse and then rounded it and bent down for a closer look at the animal's injured leg.

A low whistle slid from between his teeth as he saw the broken skin he had not been able to see before from the opposite side of the animal and the broken and bloody shard of bone that protruded through the ragged opening in the flesh.

He stood up, his teeth grinding together. A muscle in his jaw jumped. The horse swung its head around to stare inquisitively at him with its huge brown eyes. He put out a hand and the horse shied. He spoke to it. He put his hand on its neck, patted it, ran his fingers through the animal's thick mane, drew his gun, placed it beside the horse's head, cocked it, fired. He quickly stepped back out of the way as the sorrel's body fell heavily to the ground. It lay there twitching violently for several minutes before it gave one final convulsive lurch which was followed immediately by total immobility.

Whoever had this horse, he thought, is either unarmed or out of ammunition or too squeamish to have done what needed doing. Endicott? Maybe. Maybe not.

He swung into the saddle and went galloping west-
ward.

As he rode, he continued cutting for sign and soon
found himself following the plain trail of a man on foot.
From time to time, he looked up toward the Sierra Nevada range ahead of him but he saw nothing moving. The
land across which he was traveling was far from level and
it was dotted with trees, some of them growing in thick
glades, so the fact that he saw no one did not unduly
disturb him. The person he was trailing, he reasoned,
could be in among the trees or down in a grade that was
deep enough to hide him from sight.

As he rode on he came to a terraced expanse of granite
that was composed of a series of soft, rounded ledges that
made traveling difficult and trailing impossible. No footprints showed on the unyielding granite slabs. No vegetation grew on them that might reveal by a bent bough or
broken twig the fact that someone had passed that way.
Sutton swore. He drew rein and looked around him. The
stratified rock formation stretched out in a seemingly endless panorama ahead of and on both sides of him. Reluctantly, he admitted to himself that he had lost the trail.

Maybe, he speculated silently, I can pick it up once I'm
past this part of the country.

But when he came to the end of the glacier-eroded
area, he could find no sign of the person he was trailing.
He rode both to the right and the left for some distance
beyond it but turned up nothing. He shrugged, accepting
the fact that he had lost the trail, turned his horse, and
continued riding west, hoping as he did so that he would
pick up the trail somewhere up ahead.

But he did not. Instead, he spotted a town in the distance that seemed to be composed of buildings which
were little more than one-story shacks and shanties. He
rode on until he came to the broad path that served the

town as its only street and then rode down it, noting the empty buildings that seemed to have been, judging by their decrepit appearance—many were rotting where they stood, to have been abandoned years ago, leaving the place a silent, wind-swept ghost town.

A wooden sign bearing the painted words, PROSPECT and POPULATION 37 tilted at a crazy angle in front of a building which bore another painted sign: TOWN HALL.

Silver, he thought. Or maybe gold. One or the other's no doubt what lured the thirty-seven souls here to make the mining town they named Prospect. He wondered who the people had been and where they had gone. The West, he thought, it's full of ghost towns like this here one and every last one of them's haunted by men and women with dead dreams in their eyes and no hope left in their hearts.

A sharp, snapping sound caused him to stiffen and turn swiftly in the saddle as he tried to determine where the sound that he thought had come from behind him had originated. He sat in his saddle, not moving a muscle, listening, as the wind lifted his long hair and blew dust into his eyes. He rubbed his eyes which had began to water and then managed to blink the dust away. Suddenly, he thought he saw movement. Or had he only imagined it? There was a sign on a building not far from him, its weathered words unreadable, which hung by a single chain, its other one rusted through. It swayed in the wind, casting shadows that scurried along the ground beneath it. Was that what he had seen out of the corner of his eyes? Moving shadows sired by the sun and the swaying sign?

He waited but he heard nothing more, saw nothing else —if indeed he had seen anything substantial in the first place.

He turned around and moved the dun out. The animal

had gone no more than ten yards when Sutton heard it again—that distinctive snapping sound he had heard before. The sound of weakened wood breaking. Like maybe a rotten floorboard somebody had stepped on, he thought.

Leaving his horse with its reins trailing, he drew his forty-five and started slowly back down the street, his eyes darting from right to left as he surveyed the area in search of what—or who—had made the sounds he had heard. He saw no one and heard nothing more. His eyes fell on the building with the broken glass front, the shards of which bore the whitewashed letters: *loon.*

Out of the corner of his eyes he had seen movement within the building that had once been a saloon. He was sure he had. No, he admitted to himself, I'm not all that sure I saw anything at all. It might be that the light's playing tricks on me. Or could be the wind roving through these ramshackle buildings makes things inside them move.

Nevertheless, despite his uncertainty, or perhaps, because of it, he decided to investigate further. He made his way into the interior of the former saloon and stood just inside the door for a moment until his eyes became accustomed to the darkness. When they did, he was able to make out overturned chairs, tables thick with dust, and a bar on which a single empty glass sat which contained only more dust.

He turned swiftly to the right as he heard something slam loudly against something else, earing back the hammer of his six-gun as he did so. Then, smiling grimly to himself and relaxing when he saw what had made the sound—a broken shutter flung by the wind against the frame of a glassless window—he made his way up to the bar. He turned around to face the entrance to the saloon and braced his elbows on the bar. He placed the heel of one boot on the tarnished brass rail. He heard a faint sound behind him and was about to turn to see what had made it. But before he could do so, something struck the back of his head from behind, knocking off his hat. The blow from the unseen object set his senses spinning. His legs began to give way under him. He felt his fingers weaken, and through a haze, saw his gun fall to the floor.

A redness reeled in his brain. Swiftly, it darkened, giving way to a soundless and sightless blackness into which he swiftly slid.

Sutton regained consciousness slowly, his mind dulled, his senses unfocused. For one uneasy moment as he lay on the floor, he did not know where or even who he was. But then, like a dam bursting, images flooded his mind. The camp fire he had come upon. The injured sorrel. The ghost town and the sounds he had heard in it . . .

He opened his eyes and saw darkness that was dissipated slightly on one side of the saloon by moonlight drifting through a window. He shifted position on the floor in preparation for getting to his feet—and found that he could hardly move because ropes bound his hands and feet to the brass rail at the foot of the bar. Pain shuddered through his skull and he squeezed his eyes shut, willing it to go away. It didn't. If anything, when he again shifted position, it became worse. Trying his best to ignore it, he stared down at the ropes that his unseen attacker had looped around the rail before tying their ends to his wrists and ankles.

Then, by adroitly maneuvering his body, he was able to thrust the fingers of one hand into his boot. He withdrew the bowie knife he kept there, and gripping its hilt tightly in his right hand, he began to cut into the rope encircling his ankles.

A sharp pain suddenly shot through his left calf and on up into his thigh, a pain born of the twisted position he had been forced to assume in order to retrieve and use his knife. The pain caused his body to spasm violently in reaction to it. He twisted his leg in a way he hoped would relieve the pain. It did. But his abrupt movement caused him to drop his knife which struck the brass rail and bounced to one side.

He slid his body along the floor while simultaneously moving his hands and feet so that the ropes that bound them slid along the rail as he sought to recover his dropped knife. But both ropes suddenly snagged on a thick metal upright supporting and encircling the brass rail. He found he could go no farther. His knife lay tantalizingly on the floor in the moonlight just beyond his reach.

He strained as hard as he could, even though he knew the effort would be unavailing. The knife lay far beyond the tips of his grasping fingers. He muttered an oath and kicked out in fury. His boots struck the rail.

He stared at it. Had it moved when his boots had hit it? He thought it had. Quickly he bent down and squinted at it while simultaneously running his fingers along it. When he felt a ragged spot on the rail, hope flared within him. He backed up, his buttocks sliding along the floor until his bound feet and hands were stretched taut in front of him. He began to pull on the ropes with both his hands and feet, his eyes fixed on the two ropes encircling the rail. He saw the rail give slightly and then slowly begin to bend. He continued pulling and the rail continued bending, pointing toward him now like the base of a wide-angled V. Another minute's worth of strenuous pulling and the rail broke at the precise spot where he had felt the ravages of corrosion had weakened it.

He toppled over backwards, stirring up dust. Then he was scuttling along the floor, his hands and feet still bound —but free of the brass rail. He seized his bowie knife and quickly cut the rope around his ankles. Then he went to work on the rope binding his wrists. Several minutes later, he succeeded in severing it.

Booting his knife again, he got to his feet and retrieved his hat which he clapped back on his head. He picked up his still cocked gun and headed for the door of the saloon.

He halted halfway to it. Careful, he cautioned himself. The sonofabitch who knocked me senseless and tied me up might still be around here someplace. He moved more slowly toward the door, the gun in his hand giving him a comforting sense of security. He listened carefully at the door before stepping cautiously outside where his dun stood, one more shadow in a night that was alive with them.

He saw nothing. He heard nothing.

He was on his way to his dun when he suddenly stopped. Something had caught his eye. What, he wondered. Something more sensed than clearly seen. Whatever it was had caused him to go rigid because he had perceived it, although subconsciously, as a signal of potential danger. He slowly turned, his eyes scanning the dilapidated buildings on both sides of the street, his ears probing the night for sounds. At first—nothing. Then—something.

He saw smoke rising from a tin stovepipe jutting from the roof of a building diagonally across the street from where he stood. The smoke sliced grayly through the white crescent moon that was riding high in the starry sky.

Smoke? In an uninhabited ghost town?

His teeth ground together. Prospect's sure enough a ghost town. But uninhabited? That's what I thought it was when I rode in. But it turns out—looks like—I was wrong.

He crossed the street, his finger tightening on the trigger of his forty-five. He pressed his back against the front wall of the building from which the smoke was coming and eased along until he reached a broken window. Carefully, he peered through the window. He saw nothing in the room. He darted past the window and then eased through the front door and into the large room that was filled with decrepit tables and chairs. Hanging in a window on one side of the building was a rotten gingham curtain that once had been blue but was now a cobwebbed black.

If it's him in here, he thought, thinking of whoever had felled him so sneakily earlier, I'll do for him he promised himself, moving toward a door at the rear of the room. When he reached it, he halted and listened but could hear nothing. Making up his mind, he moved swiftly, in what seemed to be a single fluid motion into the room that was lighted by a coal-oil lamp which had a smoke-blackened glass chimney, his gun thrust out aggressively.

A faint feeling of foolishness washed over him when he saw that the kitchen in which he found himself was empty and he had not got, as he had planned to do, the drop on whoever might be in it because no one was.

Where the hell, he asked himself, is he? Or her? He stared at the cast-iron stove on which a pot sat bubbling and sending tendrils of steam and a tantalizing aroma into the air. Through the stove's only partially shuttered grate, he could see flames consuming lengths of wood. He had found the source of the smoke. But where was the one who had built the fire?

"Howdy."

Sutton spun around on his heels at the sound of the greeting and found himself facing an elderly gnome of a man who had a gray grizzled beard, sparkling blue eyes, a cheerful smile on his face, and an armload of wood.

"Saw you sneak in here when I was around back," the

man said. "Wondered why you did. So I snuck in after you. Are you fixing to shoot me?"

Sutton looked down at his gun and then up again at the unarmed oldster who had stuck his thumbs in his galluses and was still staring at him, his blue eyes still sparkling and his smile still cheerful.

"I thought Prospect was supposed to be a ghost town," he told the stranger.

"Oh, it is, it definitely is that. Yes, sir, you've hit it. Prospect's been a ghost town for close to ten years."

"You're the second ghost I've run into in it since sundown."

"Who was the other one? But wait—don't get me wrong. *I* ain't no haunt. Was the other one?"

"To tell you the truth, old-timer, I don't rightly know," Sutton answered, holstering his gun. "I never saw who hit me."

"Somebody hit you?"

Sutton explained what had happened to him shortly after his arrival in Prospect.

"You say you're trailing this fella, Endicott. How come, if you don't mind my being a bit nosy."

Sutton told him.

"Young pups like this here Endicott fellow you're out after sure do seem to get themselves all bolluxed up when it comes to courting these days. In my time, things was a whole lot different. We didn't hold with such foolishness. We took the bull by the horns and the first thing you knew we had grandkids. *Whoops!*"

Sutton's hand went for his gun again as the old man lunged toward him. As the man went harmlessly past him, his hand dropped to his side and he turned around to find the man easing the pot over to the cold side of the stove.

"Almost boiled over," he declared. "Dumplings," he said, pointing to the pot. "You like dumplings?"

Sutton's mouth began to water. He nodded.

"You'll find tin plates up in that cupboard over there. You can rinse 'em off with water from the pump at the sink. Eating irons is in that drawer next the stove. Set a couple of places in there,"—he pointed to the room from which both he and Sutton had entered the kitchen—"and we'll have us a dumpling or two. They may not be as light as air but they're lighter than lead, that much I can promise you. By the way, son, what's your monicker—if you don't mind an old man's prying?"

"Sutton. What's yours?"

"Kemp."

Later, as the two men sat at a table in what Kemp told Sutton had been the dining room of a restaurant when Prospect was a silver-mining boomtown with the coal-oil lamp flickering between them, Sutton asked him what he was doing in Prospect.

"I got in about an hour after sunset. I'm on my way up to the Bailey Logging Camp with a load of supplies. I come from Old Town due east of here. I generally stop along the way and spend the night here in Prospect. I've been supplying the timber beasts up at Bailey's for years now. It's not a bad business but—"

Sutton swallowed the dumpling he had forked into his mouth a moment earlier. "Timber beasts?"

For a moment, Kemp's face looked blank. Then, "You never heard them words before?" When Sutton shook his head, Kemp continued, "That's the monicker they give to any poor misguided soul who takes it upon himself to work the woods, whether he be a faller, a peeler, a river pig, a skid greaser—whatever job he does."

Sutton frowned. "What you're talking, Kemp, it sounds like a brand-new language to me."

"I reckon it does—to somebody who's never worked the woods. A faller, now he's a feller who cuts down trees.

Peelers strip bark. River pigs, they work the river to keep the logs free, so they don't jam up, and skid greasers do just what their monicker says they do—they grease the skids with animal fat or rancid butter, or even water if they ain't got nothing better to hand, so the oxen can drag their loads of logs real easy down the skid road to the river."

Sutton speared another dumpling and forked it into his mouth.

"The lumber business is booming," Kemp commented happily between mouthfuls of food. "Which is good for me and my supply business. It's good too for all the fiddle-footed jaspers wandering around looking for work. Bailey's bull of the woods—" When Kemp saw Sutton look questioningly at him, he explained, "The bull of the woods, he's the logging boss—the camp foreman. Anyway, like I was saying, the lumber business is booming and to get enough men to work for logging Bailey's bull of the woods—the fellow's name is Terrence Mulroy—he went and posted notices in every town for miles around offering top dollar. Men have been flocking to the camp from as far away as Salt Lick and New Town and Brewster and—"

Sutton didn't hear the rest of what Kemp was saying, because he was focusing on the fact that Bailey's bull of the woods had posted notices offering lucrative work in a number of towns—including Brewster where Aaron Endicott had stayed briefly with his sister and brother-in-law.

"How far off from here is Bailey?" he asked Kemp who had fallen silent.

"It's pretty far up on the slopes of the high Sierra where the timber grows the thickest. I expect to get up there sometime late tomorrow afternoon. Why do you ask?"

"I was thinking of riding along with you if you wouldn't mind."

"Glad to have you, son. The one thing I can't abide about my job is how lonesome it gets making these long hauls from Old Town all the way up the mountain which after a while make a man feel like he's halfway to heaven. You're more than welcome to join me." Kemp paused and gave Sutton a sharp look. "But what about this Endicott fellow you're after? You've decided to forget about him, have you?"

"Nope." Far from it, Sutton thought.

"You think maybe he might be up at Bailey's, do you?" Kemp asked shrewdly.

"Yep." Bailey's lumber camp was, Sutton thought, as likely a place as any to find a man who was headed in that direction, loved the outdoors, and was in need of a job to support himself.

FIVE

"How're you doing, Sutton," Kemp asked the next day as he drove his wagon, to which Sutton's horse was tied, up one more steep, rocky slope and then down into one equally rocky valley.

Sutton, holding tight to the bouncing wagon's seat to keep from falling off, replied, "Well, Kemp, to tell you the truth, this rough ride of ours has got me feeling like a horse that's been rode hard and put away wet."

Kemp guffawed and clucked to his team. The wagon wheels struck huge rocks with an impact that savagely jarred Sutton's spine but Kemp, apparently unmindful of the bone-dislocating jolts and bouncing, began to whistle a sprightly tune.

Around Sutton the wind whispered in the green needles of the pines, an eerie accompaniment to Kemp's whistling. A mile farther along, Sutton saw a doe wandering through a sun-dappled glade and watched as she, becoming aware of the wagon's approach, deftly and firmly nosed her two fawns into a copse of willow trees where all three stood perfectly still as they watched the wagon pass by them.

Everywhere Sutton looked, he saw huge rock formations of every conceivable size and shape that had been formed either by glaciers in ages past or pressure inside the rocks themselves. Some reflected the light of the sun; some seemed to absorb it. Out of cracks and crevices among the rocks grew stunted junipers, their branches all bent at right angles to their trunks and all pointing in the same direction as a result of the endless battering they received from the restless wind that roamed the mountains.

Sutton glanced at the sky and saw the young hawk that was soaring so gracefully on an updraft in it, seeming at times as it changed course to fly right into the face of the blazing sun. As the wagon rumbled on through a meadow made bright by Indian paintbrush and blue flax, Sutton continued to hold tightly to the seat. When the wagon began to climb a rock-strewn slope, its team snorting with the effort and occasionally backsliding, he gripped even more firmly the swaying seat beneath him. Ahead of and above him towered a jagged series of snow-covered peaks and off to his left tumbled a stream full of rapids that had been born of the runoff from those same peaks, its thunder momentarily silencing the creaking of the wagon.

He silently pointed out to Kemp a tiny alpine chipmunk that was perched on a slanted slab of granite as it went about the serious business of separating the seeds from the pinecones it had gathered.

"He's wasted his time," Kemp commented and then he pointed skyward.

Sutton looked up just in time to see a hawk come plummeting out of the sky.

"Got him!" Kemp cried as the hawk pounced upon the chipmunk and then soared back up into its airy domain, its doomed catch clutched in its claws.

After making a meager nooning on an exposed ledge where the hot sun kept at bay the chill in the almost frosty air, they continued their journey. By mid-afternoon they were driving, with Sutton now in control of the team, through a forest composed principally of ponderosa and Jeffrey pines.

The darker ponderosa pines with their layered bark

seemed in appearance to be distant cousins of the lighter Jeffreys with their deeply fissured bark.

"We've not got too much farther to go," Kemp declared. "This here's the lower edge of the Bailey lands. Farther along there's white pine with some lodgepole and sugar pines thrown in for good measure."

The sun, although far from setting yet, had slid out of sight behind a ridge up ahead of the wagon, its light starkly outlining the tops of a stand of ponderosa pines that seemed to spear the cloudless golden sky, when Kemp chuckled, pointed, and announced, "There's the trail that leads straight up to the camp."

The trail Kemp had pointed out, Sutton saw, came to an abrupt end—or did it begin—about forty yards ahead of them. It was heavily rutted, and Sutton estimated, a good sixteen feet wide.

Sutton headed for it, and once on it, made better time because of the absence of rocks. But the ruts were nearly as much of a problem as the rocks had been. Sutton noted the countless stumps of felled trees sprouting like flat-topped toadstools throughout the area.

He saw men in the distance moving through the trees like shadows. One of them, seeing the wagon, raised an arm and shouted a greeting. Kemp cheerfully returned both the man's wave and greeting. They emerged finally in a vast clearing that was bordered on one side by plank tables and benches and on the other by a series of buildings. Here and there in the clearing a few trees still grew —for shade, Sutton supposed, their spreading branches dancing in the wind that never seemed to stop blowing down the mountainside. Near one of the trees was a squat structure built of small stones and topped with a partially rusted iron grill.

"In midsummer like it is now," Kemp remarked, "the boys like to eat outdoors unless it's raining or snowing or the wind's strong enough to blow a man down. Pull up over there."

Sutton pulled up in front of the building Kemp had designated and threw on the brake. As he stepped gingerly down upon a wheel and from there to the ground, favoring his bruised buttocks and legs which were the result of the rocky ride up to the lumber camp, Kemp also got down from the wagon and declared, with an expansive wave of both arms, "This is about the closest a man can come to heaven without having to die first. Smell the air, Sutton."

"It's real pure and sweet."

"That it is, son. And why shouldn't it be? It's the same air the angels breathe, we're that high up."

"You said something before about snow—or did my ears twist out of shape what you said?"

"You heard me right. It snows at least once a month—sometimes more—up this high every summer. There's nearly always a nip in the air."

Sutton felt it—had been feeling it for some time.

"Hallo there you old sonofagun," Kemp called out to a man who had just emerged from the building in front of which Sutton had parked the wagon. "Long time no see, Landers."

"That was a mercy," laconically commented the lean and mustachioed man who stood in the doorway of the building. "I mean it was a tender mercy not having to lay eyes on you, Kemp."

"You could do a lot worse, Landers."

"Impossible."

"Some of these timber beasts you've got up here are so repulsive they could blind any man who dares look at them."

"I still say I'd rather look on the devil himself than a

plug-ugly old codger such as yourself, Kemp," Landers persisted, a scowl on his face.

Kemp shook his head in mock chagrin as he gave Sutton an exasperated glance. "I've about had me enough of this palaver, son. This here sour-faced fellow's the camp cook and only a fool argues with a skunk, a mule, or a cook."

Sutton caught both the sly grin Kemp gave him and the secretive wink Landers gave him. These two, he thought, it's clear they're old friends.

"This here feller," Kemp said to Landers, "goes by the name of Sutton. Sutton meet Landers, the meanest cook this side of California."

The two men shook hands and then Sutton asked, "Are there any other lumber camps anywheres about?"

"Not between here and Russell's which is over on the other side of the mountains in California," Landers answered. "Over there they fall the big redwoods."

"Is there by any chance any other place around here where a man might get himself gainfully employed?"

Landers shook his head.

Kemp said, "If it's a job you're looking for, Sutton, you could do worse than hire on here at Bailey's. The pay's good though the eats is awful." He ducked and laughed as Landers took a playful swing at him. "That's how come Bailey's is notorious for winding up with so many short stake men," Kemp added and then let out a loud, "Owwooo!" as Landers landed a punch on his shoulder.

"What's a short stake man?" Sutton inquired.

"A timber beast who hires on and is gone in two, three days—maybe a week," Landers answered. "And don't you pay Kemp no attention. He's been a liar since the day he was born. Any man who hires on here, why, I'll feed him so's he's fat and sassy in no time a'tall."

"Enough of your big windies, Landers," Kemp said gruffly. "Help me unload my wagon so I can head for

Bailey where I'm bent on buying myself another subscription to *Godey's Lady's Book*."

Sutton, wondering why a man like Kemp would want to buy a subscription to *Godey's Lady's Book* bade the man and his friend Landers goodbye. He freed his horse from the rear of Kemp's wagon and then surveyed the lumber camp which was almost completely deserted. The only men he saw were one who was seated in front of one of the bunkhouses with his bandaged bare foot propped up in front of him on a three-legged stool and a second one who had clothes soaking in a wooden tub full of hot water which he was vigorously pounding with a thick stick in an effort to rid them of dirt.

After tying his dun to a tree, he made his way over to the man who was washing clothes. "I'm a stranger in these parts," he told the man. "Name's Sutton. Been trying to find a friend of mine who wrote me he had him a job in some lumber camp or other. I just came from Russell's but he wasn't to be found there. Fact is, I suspect he may be a short stake man and as such might have shown up here—be still here maybe. His name's Aaron Endicott. Have you seen or heard of him?"

"No," the man answered bluntly without raising his eyes. "But that doesn't mean he's not here. This place is stacked to the rafters with all kinds of men whose names I don't know."

Sutton made his way over to the man who was sitting and sunning his bandaged foot. He told the invalid the same story he had just told the other man.

"Aaron Endicott," the man repeated when Sutton had finished speaking. "No, I can't say as the name's the least bit familiar to me. But then lots of fellers out here in the woods don't use their real names for one reason or another. Some of them are running from the law or a woman or, far worse, themselves. Nobody asks questions. It ain't always healthy to. Your friend might have changed his name."

Sutton gave the man a physical description of Endicott. "Haven't seen such a feller, sorry."

Sutton returned to the man who was still doing his washing and this time he described Endicott but again he received a negative answer. He made his way back the way he had come and sat down on a smooth tree stump. Maybe, he thought, Endicott's on his way to California to find a job and start a new life. Or maybe he changed his mind and turned around and headed back to Virginia City and the love of his life, Violet Wilson. Which, if he did, leaves me perched high and dry and wasting my time out here in the woods.

He was on the verge of returning to where Kemp was helping Landers unload supplies from the wagon when a noisy horde of men came crashing out of the surrounding forest carrying broadaxes, crosscut saws, spouted and corked metal and glass containers, climbing irons, and wooden mallets. He scanned their faces eagerly, searching for Endicott.

As the men, some of them singing, some of them looking dour and defeated, began to disappear into the bunkhouse or sat down in clusters on the wooden benches to talk or play cards, he got up and wandered hopefully among them. As more and more men streamed out of the forest with the tools of their trade in their hands or over their shoulders, he continued his search.

Later, as the flow of men subsided to a trickle, he glanced at the wagon which was almost completely empty now. Should he ride partway back the way he had come with Kemp when the supplier left camp, which he guessed would be sometime the next day? Or should he continue heading west toward California?

He pushed his thoughts aside as he saw a man emerge

from the woods with a broadax over his shoulder. Sutton stared at the man thinking: there's something familiar about that jasper. But what? As the man suddenly turned and headed back into the woods, Sutton realized why he had thought that the stranger had looked vaguely familiar to him.

His beard's gone, he thought. So's his mustache. But that's him. To make sure, he got up and sprinted after the man he believed to be the now clean-shaven Aaron Endicott. He searched through the woods but could turn up no trace of him. Finally, he gave up his search. He'll be back, he confidently told himself. And when he does, I'll be right here to keep an eye on him like Violet Wilson's paying me to do.

Now that my job's half finished, he thought as he headed back to where Kemp stood beside his almost empty wagon, I've got to see to it that no harm comes to Endicott till Violet can come claim her best beloved and take him off my hands. To do that, he decided he would have to get himself a job in the lumber camp.

But first he had to take care of another important task— one he believed he would need Kemp's help to accomplish. He headed back to Kemp's wagon where he asked the teamster when he planned to head back to Old Town.

"Sometime tomorrow, I reckon," Kemp answered. "Why?"

"Is there mail delivery in Old Town where you come from?"

"There is."

"If I give you a letter, will you mail it for me when you get back home to Old Town?"

"Sure, I will, only I don't know why you want to bother going such a roundabout way to get a letter delivered."

"I don't follow you."

"You can go to Bailey and mail it there. The mail for all

the camp's timber beasts comes there and the mail they send heads east, west, everywhere from Bailey."

"I'm obliged to you for the information, Kemp."

Sutton went to his dun, freed it, swung into the saddle, and rode north through the woods, heading for the town of Bailey.

He heard it before he saw it. Shouts and laughter from the town echoed through the woods as darkness fell and he approached the town. A shot sounded. A woman screamed. A dog barked.

He rode into the town that was a jumble of plank buildings placed in a ragged double line that ran from south to north. From one hung an American flag and a sign that read: YALE HOTEL. Empty beer barrels were stacked in front of another one that had a sign that said simply: SALOON. Stumps of trees sprouted in front of and between the buildings.

Sutton drew rein in front of a tarpaper shack next door to the Sierra Mercantile Company. Leaving his horse tied to a hitchrail, he stepped up to the blackboard that hung on the shack's door and read the message that someone had chalked upon it.

Wanted by Bailey Logging Camp
4 buckers $3.00 per day
4 peelers $2.50 per day
2 fallers $3.75 per day
7 choker setters $2.00 per day
Inquire inside

Noting the shack's padlocked door, he made up his mind to return in the morning and apply for one of the jobs listed on the blackboard.

He went inside the Sierra Mercantile Company and asked the clerk behind the counter for a pencil and some paper. After paying for both items, he made his way over to the saloon where he ordered whiskey.

"One dollar," the bar dog growled after pouring his drink.

Sutton eyed the man with disbelief. "A dollar for a drink? Did I hear you right?"

"You heard me right. Things are expensive around here. That's because timber beasts can pay high prices." The bar dog held out his hand.

Sutton paid for the drink and then downed it. He was about to leave the saloon when a woman appeared out of nowhere to stand by his side.

She wore a print cotton day dress that was slightly faded and a white pillbox hat perched on her hair which was pinned on top of her head. Her face was round and her green eyes had, Sutton thought, a flat look about them as if she wasn't really present.

She gave him a tired smile that he thought might have been practiced in front of a mirror and said, "I just know you're the intellectual type. Am I right or am I wrong, big fellow?"

"I reckon you're wrong, Miss. I've had little or no schooling."

"But you're smart," she countered, wagging a playful finger in his face and smiling even more enthusiastically. "I can always spot the smart ones. They've got a keen look about them—like you have." The woman thrust a hand into a canvas bag she was carrying and came up with a dog-eared and year-old copy of *Godey's Lady's Book* which she displayed for Sutton. "This magazine is simply full of food for intellectual thought."

Something stirred in Sutton's memory. Kemp, he thought. He said he was coming here to Bailey and he was bent on buying another subscription to *Godey's Lady's Book.*

"If you want to buy a subscription," the woman was saying, "you can come along back to my room in the hotel with me and sign the appropriate papers." She hooked her arm in Sutton's and pressed her body against his. "My name's Emma. What's yours?"

He told her.

"I like the name Luke," she cooed in his ear as she tightened her grip on his arm. "I like *you*."

Sutton turned his head when he heard his name called and saw Kemp standing in the doorway of the saloon and beaming at him. Seconds later, Kemp was shaking his hand while simultaneously patting Emma on the buttocks.

Are you buying what this lovely lady's selling, Sutton?" he asked. Without waiting for an answer, he continued, "The sad fact that they don't let working girls into the lumber camp or even let them ply their trade here in town hasn't stopped Emma, as you can plainly see, Sutton. She's taken to pretending what she's got to sell is magazine subscriptions, when the truth of the matter is she's got only herself to sell and I for one am always willing to buy. How about you?"

Before Sutton could reply, Emma began to drag him toward the door. On the way to it, she called back over her shoulder to Kemp, "Don't you go away, honey. I'll be back before long."

The following morning, as he sat in the hotel room he had rented after leaving Emma, Sutton wrote a letter to Violet Wilson. In it he told her he had located Endicott and he promised her he would see to it that the man came to no harm during the time it would take Violet to get to the lumber camp. He also told her she could stay in Bailey's Yale Hotel until she and Endicott were ready to leave the area. He dated and signed the letter, addressed it to

Violet in care of Adele Fenton in Virginia City, and then took it to the Mercantile Company which also served as the local post office.

Then he went next door and pounded on the door of the tarpaper shack.

When he heard muffled sounds coming from inside the building, he pounded again, harder this time. The door was finally eased open by a man who was wearing long johns, and incongruously, a pair of plaid galluses wrapped around his neck.

"I'm looking for work," Sutton told the man who grumbled wordlessly and then beckoned him inside.

"What kind of work?" the man asked him.

"In the woods—at Bailey's Logging camp."

"I know that. That's all I handle here. But what kind of work? As a bucker, a peeler, a choker setter—what?"

Sutton recalled the time Kemp had explained to him the meaning of some of the lumber camp lingo—what a faller was, for example, and since the job of faller paid the highest of any listed on the blackboard outside, he made up his mind in a hurry.

"I see you're in need of two fallers. Well, you're looking at one of them." He was prepared to field any questions that might come concerning his professional experience as a tree-cutter—actually his lack of it—but no such questions were asked of him.

"That will cost you two dollars," declared the man as he casually removed the galluses from around his neck and dropped them to the floor.

"You mean I got to pay you for the privilege of working?"

"I'm not in business for my health."

"I reckon I'll just mosey on down to Bailey's and hire on there—save myself some money by doing this direct."

The man shook his head. "Things don't work that way.

Bailey pays me to do his hiring for him. Nobody down there will hire you."

Sutton paid the two dollars and was given a piece of paper on which the man had written Sutton's name, the per diem wage rate, and the word "faller." Pocketing the paper, he left the shack and returned to the Mercantile where he freed his dun from the hitchrail in front of the building and then led the animal to the nearby livery.

There he bought some oats and barley which he placed in a feed bin. As his horse hungrily began to eat the grain, he removed his gear from the animal and rubbed it down. He shook out his blanket and when the dun had consumed the last of the grain, he put his gear back on the horse and led it from the livery. Once out-side, he swung into the saddle and rode south.

When he got back to camp, he sought out Landers and asked him where he could find Terrence Mulroy, Bailey's bull of the woods.

"Mulroy's got most of the men working up in the northeast falling sugar pine. You fixing to go to work for him?"

"I am. Thanks for the information." Sutton tied his horse to a tree and made his way into the woods where there was little sunshine and an aromatic dampness drifted in the cool air.

He had been walking for only minutes when he heard sounds up ahead of him. They were faint and tended to blend with one another, but as Sutton continued walking, he was able to distinguish the thwack of axes and the rasp of saws, clanking chains, and then the crackling that preceded the crash as a tree toppled and hit the ground with a thunderous impact.

When he reached the area where men were scrambling around and over fallen trees and shouting to one another while busily wielding the tools of their trade, he asked the first man he met where Mulroy was to be found.

Instead of answering him, the man seized Sutton by the arm and went running west with him in tow.

"What—" Sutton began, shaking himself free of the man.

"Didn't you hear that tree talking back there?" the man asked him.

"Trees don't talk," a somewhat shaken Sutton shot back.

"It's easy to tell you're a greenhorn. Listen!"

Sutton listened and heard a man shout, "Timber! Down the hill!" and then he heard the sharp crackling sound as the last of a towering sugar pine's fibers shattered and the giant tree leaned and then came crashing down to the ground not far from where he had stood when he had first spoken to the man beside him.

"Whew!" he breathed. "Mister, I sure am glad you got me out of there while there was still enough time to get."

"You're new here, aren't you?"

"My first day."

"Well, take some friendly advice from an old-timer who's been a timber beast for close to ten years. Keep your eyes—and especially your ears—wide open. You don't and you're liable to wind up killed by a tree."

"I'll be sure to do that, since it's clear it's the prudent thing to do."

"You wanted to know where to find the bull of the woods. That's Mulroy over there—that big-brisketed feller."

Sutton made his way over to Mulroy and introduced himself, pulling the piece of paper the man at the employment agency had given him from his pocket and handing it to the foreman.

Mulroy glanced at it and then at Sutton. "How much did that shark that runs the slave shop charge you?"

"Two dollars."

Mulroy spat a brown stream of tobacco juice. "You should have come straight to me and saved yourself that shark's fee."

"I told him that's what I intended to do when he told me he was going to charge me two bucks for the job, only he said Bailey hired him to hire men to work here. He said it was the only way I could get to work here—by going through him."

"He lied to you." Mulroy glanced at the paper. "So you're a faller. Had much experience?"

"Some," Sutton responded, although he was pretty sure that his experience at cutting down trees back on his homeplace in Texas was not exactly the kind of experience Mulroy had in mind.

"Where'd you work last?"

Sutton was sure Mulroy would not be impressed by an honest answer to the question which would have to be: "In California—as a bounty hunter" so, recalling that the nearest lumber camp was named Russell's according to Landers, he lied, "I spent a month at Russell's."

"See those two fallers working over there? Spell them. I'll be keeping an eye on you, Sutton. If you do good, I'll keep you. If you don't, you can go on back to Russell's—or any other place that'll have you."

"Fair enough." Sutton headed for the two men who were working both ends of a ten-foot crosscut saw. He relieved one of them and began to work his end of the saw when the man he had relieved called for a halt. When the crosscut saw was removed from the cut, the man proceeded to drive wedges into the cut to keep the saw's blade from binding. Then, he gave the signal to proceed.

Sutton put his weight into his work and before long he began to feel his muscles tightening and then beginning to ache severely. When the man he had relieved took over for the man at the other end of the saw from Sutton and the sawing continued, the wedges began to fall out as the cut was steadily deepened.

A moment later, the faller at the other end of the saw gave Sutton a signal. Both men pulled the saw from the cut and stepped quickly back as the peculiar cracking sound Sutton had heard before again reached his ears and the faller with whom he had been working cupped his hands around his mouth and yelled, *"Timber! Down the hill!"*

Sutton arched his back and pressed his fingers into the base of his spine in an effort to relieve the soreness he was experiencing there as the tree crashed to the ground and was immediately pounced upon by a team of peelers who began to strip the bark from it with their sharp-edged peeling bars.

"You'll get over it," said the faller Sutton had just been working with when he saw the way Sutton was kneading the muscles in his arms and legs in an attempt to relieve the cramps that had seized them. "You'll loosen up in time."

"It's a comfort to hear that," Sutton said with a wry smile. "I hope I can believe it."

"I know right now it's hard to believe, but you'll be fit as a fiddle in a few days, ready and willing to take on even a man like Paul Bunyan, should he put in an appearance."

"You heard the latest about old Paul?" inquired the faller's companion.

The faller who had been talking to Sutton winked at him and whispered, "Svenson never tires of making up tall tales about Paul Bunyan."

"I was up in Bailey last week," the man named Svenson declared, taking a pinch of snuff from a small tin and placing it in his left nostril. "The man at the Mercantile Company there told me Paul come by to buy a pair of boots and he had to special-order the extra-large size. To get them to the Mercantile, the boot-maker had to hire two flatbed wagons to haul them—one boot to a wagon, they was that big."

Not to be outdone, the other faller asked, "Did you boys ever hear how Paul and his blue ox, Babe, broke the granddaddy of all logjams up in the Lake States? No? Well, it went like this if my memory serves me right. Paul and his crew were driving a big bunch of logs down the Wisconsin River when the logs up and jammed on them. Those logs were piled up two-hundred-feet high at the head and they were backed up for a mile on the river. Well, the crew was doing their damnedest to break the jam, only they couldn't. By the time Paul got to the head of the jam with Babe, he whispered in his ear and Babe went and stood in the river smack in front of the jam. Paul —he was standing on the bank—he shot Babe with a 303 Savage Rifle.

"The ox thought it was flies biting him and started to switch his tail. Well, believe it or not, that ox switching his tail forced the Wisconsin River to flow backwards and eventually the jam was broken."

Sutton, thinking fast, asked, "Did you fellows ever hear about the fine vittles Paul Bunyan served at a logging camp he once ran out in the redwood forests of California?"

Both men looked at him with amused anticipation as they shook their heads.

"He fed his men to a fare-thee-well, folks say," Sutton continued. "One day he spread his tarpaulin on the ground so it'd look like a lake. Before long he'd caught himself a flock of ducks by folding up the tarp's four corners when the ducks landed on it. He cooked them up and served them to his crew along with orders of corn on the cob the size of a man's forearm. They say those ears had kernels on them as big as buns."

"I heard about that time," Svenson said—to Sutton's complete surprise, since Sutton had just made up the story on the spur of the moment. "At the meal you're talking about they say Paul served mountains of cream puffs, each one of which was as big as a squash—bigger, some say."

"The carrots Paul raised in his kitchen garden grew so big, he used to have to hire a full crew of stump pullers to harvest them," interjected the other faller with a smile, apparently unwilling to have his imagination outclassed by those of his coworkers.

Sutton, rising to the implicit challenge offered by the rampant imaginations of his two companions, came up with, "Paul, when he cooked flapjacks, used a griddle that was a good seven-blocks long."

"It was heated by a two-acre brushfire," Svenson announced.

"And damn if it weren't greased by ten timber beasts skating across it with slabs of bacon strapped to their boots," Sutton declared with a straight, almost solemn, face.

The two fallers facing him couldn't help themselves. Both men collapsed in happy helpless laughter. A moment later, so did Sutton.

When all three men had recovered, Svenson suggested that they get back to work.

But before they could do so, a whistle shrieked.

Svenson told Sutton, "That means it's noon. Time for dinner. Let's go."

Sutton, on his way back to the camp with his co-workers, kept his eyes peeled but he saw no sign of Endicott among the other men who were also heading back to camp.

When he was seated at one of the plank tables and flanked by the two fallers, he scanned the faces of the men who were wolfing down mashed potatoes, roast beef, biscuits, and boiled beets. As far as he could see, Endicott was not among them. A feeling of uneasiness began to grow within him.

Turning to Svenson, he asked, "Do you by any chance happen to know a fellow who works here by the name of Aaron Endicott?"

Svenson, his mouth stuffed full of food, shook his head.

Sutton asked the other faller flanking him the same question and received the same negative response. He then proceeded to describe Endicott to both men.

Svenson said, "That sounds like one of the buckers who signed on the other day. He was a real greenhorn. He'd never worked the woods before, if you ask me. He was awful clumsy with a saw I noticed."

"Whitcomb," said the man who was seated on the far side of the faller who had just spoken. "You're talking about Bob Whitcomb."

Sutton leaned over, and speaking to the man who had just volunteered the information, he once again described Endicott for the man's benefit. "Are you sure that's the man you're calling Bob Whitcomb?"

"I'm sure," the man replied. "That was Whitcomb."

"Was?" Sutton prompted.

"Whitcomb," said the man as he sopped up gravy with a piece of biscuit, "was a short stake man. He took off right after quitting time yesterday."

"You saw him leave?" Sutton asked and the man nodded.

"Which way did he go?"

"West."

"On foot?"

"That's right. The same way he came is the way he went."

Svenson, on Sutton's left, took out his tin of snuff and offered it to Sutton who shook his head and got to his feet.

"Where are you heading in such an all-fired hurry?" Svenson asked him as he left the table.

Sutton didn't bother to answer as he headed for the spot where he had left his dun.

Behind him he heard Svenson sneeze and then say, "I thought that fellow had the look of a short stake man about him the first time I laid eyes on him."

SIX

Sutton picked up the trail of a lone man on foot when he was only a quarter mile west of the lumber camp. He was able to follow it easily, thinking that Endicott—if indeed it was Endicott's trail he was following—had made no effort to cover his tracks. Which means, he thought, either the man don't know how to hide where he'd been or he don't care to because he don't think anybody's following him.

Another thought, one that gave him encouragement to much the same degree that the plain trail he had found did, occurred to him. A man on foot, he told himself, can't make anywhere near as good time in rough country like this as can a man on a horse.

He rode on through a field that was strewn with fragments from huge, frost-cracked boulders which had long ago tumbled down into the field from the heights above. They lay like the remains of some primitive city that had fallen into ruin untold ages ago.

He rode up slopes and down them again, his sharp eyes continuously scanning the ground and surrounding vegetation for sign of his quarry. He frequently found what he was looking for with little or no trouble. A snapped branch of a young juniper bearing a black thread. Flattened grass bordered by nearly foot-high walls of upright grass. The footprints of someone who was wearing townsman's shoes, not the calked boots of a woodsman which would have left holes in the earth where boots' spikes had dug into the ground.

He was riding along a ridge when he spotted the broken ground directly ahead of him and it told him what had happened at that spot.

The edge of the ridge was broken off. It had obviously given way under the weight of the person whose footprints led up to the ragged spot and then abruptly vanished. The upturned earth at the spot was still damp, indicating to Sutton that the person who had fallen from the ridge had done so not long ago, since the sun had not yet had time to dry the newly uncovered dirt.

He got out of the saddle, and leaving his horse behind him, walked gingerly up to the spot, expecting at any moment to feel the ground begin to give way beneath his boots. When he reached the spot, he leaned over the ledge and looked down. It was not a deep drop, he was glad to see. If it had been, whoever had fallen from the ridge might have been killed. But Sutton didn't think the person was much more than bruised a bit. He came to that tentative conclusion based on his observations of the vegetation growing on the sloping wall below the ridge. Some of the vegetation was crushed, and by following the trace of broken bushes and briars, he could chart the path the person had taken as he had tumbled down the slope into the narrow gulch below.

Sutton walked back the way he had come. When he reached his horse, he carefully led it back along the ridge, keeping away from the edge. When he got down from the ridge, he made his way past the mouth of the gulch and along its twisting length until he reached the spot where the man he was trailing had fallen from the ridge up above. He hunkered down, scanning the ground around him. He spotted tracks a few feet away which told him that the man he was after was now favoring his left leg. Leading his dun, he began to follow the trail left by the limping man.

He moved through a tall growth of tangled brush, shielding his eyes with his forearm as he did so. Just as he was about to emerge from it, he first heard the sound of a branch breaking and then, not far ahead of him, he saw his quarry. He stood without moving and watched, a smile spreading slowly across his face. When the man had moved out of sight, he remained where he was, waiting and listening. Then, turning, he made his way north, traveling at a right angle to the course he had been following, still leading his dun. When he emerged from the thicket, he left his horse with its reins trailing behind him and proceeded to climb a rocky slope. When he reached its summit, he carefully made his way down the other side and around a sharp bend where he halted, surveying the scene in front of him.

It took him less than a minute to spot what he had been searching for. Drawing his six-gun, he made his way forward, and when he was directly behind the man he had been stalking, he said, "On your feet, Endicott."

Endicott, startled, turned sharply and stared up at Sutton from where he squatted, a broken tree limb clutched tightly in his right hand.

Sutton repeated his order and then added, "And drop that skull-buster you're holding."

Endicott dropped the tree limb and slowly rose until he was facing Sutton who said, "You were planning, I take it, to try to put me out of commission."

Endicott said nothing.

"How come?" Sutton asked, holstering his gun.

Endicott countered with a question of his own. "Why have you been following me?"

Instead of answering, Sutton asked, "How long have you known I've been following you?"

"Since long before my horse hurt himself."

The reply gave Sutton the answer to another question

he had on his mind, one he had not yet asked Endicott. "So it was you who jumped me back in that ghost town."

"It looks like I should have hit you harder than I did, since here you are still after me."

Sutton said nothing for a moment. Then, "You spotted me back in the lumber camp. That's why you took off."

"I certainly wasn't going to wait around until you could put a bullet in my back."

"Now what in the world gives you the idea I'm out to kill you?"

"Aren't you?"

"Nope."

"Then Dade Talbot didn't send you out to track me down?"

"Nope."

A perplexed expression came over Endicott's face. "Then who did?"

"A lady name of Violet Wilson."

"Violet!"

Sutton nodded.

"I don't understand."

"You should. She loves you. She wants you back. So for those two good reasons she hired me to find you."

"I'm not going back to Virginia City," Endicott stated heatedly. "I can't. If I do, Talbot will kill Violet. Didn't she tell you about the threat he made against her?"

"She told me."

"Then you know I can't go back. Dade Talbot will kill her if she and I—I tried to explain to her—I left her a note—"

"She doesn't want you to come back to Virginia City. And she does understand why you felt you had to do what you did. She knows you left town to protect her. But the fact of the matter is she loves you and she don't intend to let Talbot stand in the way of her having you and being

happy in the having. She plans on rejoining you. I was to
let her know where you were, if and when I caught up
with you. I've already done that. I've sent word to her that
you are—you were—in Bailey's lumber camp. I think it
would be a fine idea were you and me to mosey on back to
camp and sit tight while we wait for her to show up. Then
the pair of you can decide what your next move should be
—where you both want to go from there."

Endicott sat down on a rocky ledge. Staring up at Sutton, he shook his head and said, "I guess I've made rather
a mess of things the way I acted toward you. But I didn't
know who you were or why you were following me. I was
—I'll admit it—scared. When I first saw you and then
realized you were following me—I became even more
scared. I was sure Talbot had sent you to kill me. I could
think of no other reason to explain why you were after
me. I'm sorry for what I did to you back in that ghost
town. But maybe now you can at least understand why I
did it."

"Let's go, Endicott. It's time we were heading back to
camp."

Sutton and Endicott returned to the lumber camp late
the following day, and after conferring with Mulroy, the
bull of the woods, they were both hired again as buckers.

"I've got a full crew of fallers," Mulroy told Sutton when
Sutton asked him if he could go back to work as the faller
he had been. "You'll be a bucker for now, same as Endicott was, or you'll be nothing," Mulroy responded
bluntly.

"It's not so bad, Luke," Endicott told him as both men
made their way over to where felled trees lay haphaz-
ardly on the ground beside the flume that was used to
transport logs down the mountain. "It gets monotonous

after a while, but then so did the accounting work I used to do."

"I have to ask you something," Sutton said. "What exactly does a bucker do?"

"He cuts trees into logs of manageable length so they can be sent down that flume over there." Endicott pointed to it.

Sutton stared at the narrow wooden trough that Endicott had pointed out to him. It had slanted sides and rested on pyramidal supports as it twisted and turned its way down the mountainside. He heard the dull thudding of logs slamming against the flume's sides as they hurtled down it and he also heard the splashing and gurgling of the water which carried the logs on their rapid downmountain journey.

"The logs pile up at the end of the flume in the valley below," Endicott told him. "Wagons pick them up and haul them from there to sawmills."

Sutton went up to the flume and looked down into it at the logs that were speeding past him in the roiling stream of water the flume contained. They're moving so fast a man couldn't count them, he thought, at least too fast for this man to count.

When he heard movement behind him, he turned to find that Endicott had picked up one end of a crosscut saw and was waiting for him. He retraced his steps, gripped the other end of the long saw, and then both men began to cut into the trunk of one of the felled trees.

"You're right about the flume providing a fast trip down the mountain," Endicott commented as they sawed, their bodies bending forward and then backward with each long stroke. "When I first got here, there was a man hit by a widow-maker who—"

"What's a widow-maker?"

"A treetop or limb or even a heavy piece of bark that

can kill a man if it should fall and hit him. That's what happened to the fellow I started to tell you about. The widow-maker that struck him didn't kill him but it did break a few of his bones. There's no doctor up here in camp, so Mulroy asked for a volunteer and one of the men volunteered to take the injured man down to the nearest doctor on the flume."

"How'd he do that?"

"In one of the flat-bottomed boats Mulroy sometimes uses to send packages or messages down to the valley or to the flume tenders—men who are stationed at intervals along the length of the flume. The boat's got a V-shaped keel and a plank platform that runs from stem to stern which serves as a deck."

"Did the man make it—I mean the one who was all stove in?"

Endicott shook his head. "He died."

"What about the fellow who volunteered to take him down the flume?"

Endicott looked up at Sutton a moment after their saw cut through the tree trunk. "You're thinking he might have gotten hurt himself on the trip. Well, he didn't. Except for some bad bruises, he came out of it in one piece. Of course, he'd ridden the flume once or twice before, I heard, so I suppose he knew how to handle the boat and look out for himself."

As they started a new cut, Endicott mused, "I'm not sure Violet ought to come out here into the wilderness. I mean she's leaving her whole life behind her. She's pulling up her roots and burning her bridges."

"She struck me as a lady who knows what she's doing. I think you're wrong about her leaving her whole life behind her. *You* are her whole life, I'd say, after listening to her. And though she may be pulling up her roots like you said, there's nothing to stop her from putting down new ones wherever it is you two finally wind up. As for the burned bridges, I don't think they matter much, since she sure did seem to me to be bound and determined to go forward, not backwards."

"Maybe you're right. But I can't help feeling worried."

"Once she gets here and you've had a chance to talk to her, I reckon you'll feel better."

"To tell you the truth, on the one hand I'm worried, but on the other hand I can hardly wait to see her. Making up my mind to leave her—that was just about the hardest thing I ever did in my entire life."

"I've no doubt that's true."

"She ought to get here in a day or two, don't you think?"

"It might take her a little longer than that," Sutton said, aware of the eagerness that had brightened Endicott's tone. *He's going to find the waiting hard,* he thought. *I know I would too, were I waiting on a woman even half as lovely as Violet Wilson is.*

In the days that followed, Sutton spent his days working the woods which were noisy with the loud shouts of men and the louder thunder of trees as they were cut down and his nights in the bunkhouse to which he had been assigned, which was overcrowded, sometimes smoky due to the cast-iron stove's faulty flue, and redolent with the odors of sweat, tobacco, and coal oil.

Mulroy assigned him to various tasks. Sometimes he worked with Endicott and sometimes he did not. Most of his second day back in camp he spent swinging a peeling bar as he and the other members of the peeling crew stripped the thick bark from a seemingly endless series of redwoods. The day after that Mulroy sent him down the mountain to work as what the bull of the woods had called a "lumber herder" and which Endicott had earlier referred to as a "flume tender." One of his jobs during the day was to patrol the narrow catwalk that ran alongside the flume looking for leaks or jams. If he found a leak, he was to repair it. If he found a jam, he was to clear it quickly before the combined weight of the jammed lumber caused a section of the flume to collapse. He spent his nights in the small cabin that was the rude domain of the flume tender, where he got little or no sleep because of the constant, shrill rattling of a tin can that a previous tender had hung in the flume which indicated, as long as its racket continued, that the logs were moving along properly. Its silence alerted the tender to a logjam.

He was also required to periodically check on the condition of the spot where a portion of the flume's upper wall had been temporarily removed to let logs leave the flume at that point and pile up below it.

He spent another three days at his post before being relieved. The first thing he did upon his return to camp was to seek out Endicott. He had barely begun his search when his inquiries yielded the information that Endicott had quit his job the day before, and according to his informant, gone into Bailey after having received a message from someone in the town.

Sutton thanked the man he had been talking to and made his way over to where Mulroy was standing and talking with some of his men. "I hear Endicott's left camp," Sutton said to the bull of the woods. "I wonder, did he leave me any kind of word before he went?"

"As a matter of fact he did," Mulroy responded somewhat sullenly. "He left this for you." Pulling a crumpled envelope from his pocket, he handed it to Sutton who opened it and quickly read the letter inside.

Dear Luke

I pen these words to tell you that I received word from Violet this morning. She informs me that she has arrived at the hotel in Bailey and bids me join her there, which I shall with great delight do at once. Both Violet and I hope to see you before we must leave town. Please join us in Bailey at your earliest convenience.

Yours most sincerely,
Aaron

"I'm quitting," Sutton bluntly told Mulroy as he pocketed Endicott's letter. "I'd like to collect the pay that's due me."

With much grumbling about the trouble caused him by short-stake men, Mulroy paid Sutton the wages due him.

When he rode into Bailey later that day, he left his dun at the local livery with instructions to water and grain the animal and then went directly to the hotel where he asked the desk clerk for Endicott's room number.

When the clerk had given it to him, he made his way up the stairs and knocked on the door of room number four.

It was opened by Endicott who, the instant he recognized his visitor, broke into a broad smile and eagerly ushered Sutton into the small room.

"I gather you got the letter I left with Mulroy for you, Luke."

"I did." Sutton seated himself in a tall-backed wooden chair. "How is she?"

"Oh, Luke, Violet's wonderful. As lovely as ever. No, even lovelier. It's true what they say about absence making the heart grow fonder. Mine couldn't grow any fonder than it is at this very minute. I know she'll be glad to see you. I told her I had left word and had asked you to come here. Violet told me she always knew you would accomplish the difficult task she had set for you. I can assure you she is most grateful to you for having done so, which I find outrageously flattering."

A knock sounded at the door and Endicott practically raced to it. "But I'll let her tell you herself about how grateful she is to you." He opened the door to admit Violet Wilson, and as she swept into the room, Sutton rose to greet her.

When she saw him, she hurried up to him and surprised him by throwing her arms around him and hugging him. Before he could say a word, she drew back, released him, and exclaimed, "Luke, I am forever in your debt. And speaking of debt," she continued, reaching into the reticule she carried, "I have this for you."

Sutton took from her the five hundred dollars she handed him and pocketed it. "What plans do you and Endicott have in mind now—if you don't mind my asking such a personal question?"

"I don't mind at all," Violet replied. "Aaron and I have talked about what we should do at this point—where we should go."

"But we haven't come to any firm conclusion yet," Endicott stated.

"I suggested that we go on to California," Violet remarked.

"What made you pick California?" Sutton asked her.

"Oh, no particular reason," she answered airily with a wave of her hand. "I have heard that it is a lovely place. Warm. The Pacific ocean is there and I have never seen an ocean—except in paintings. I suppose I have more than a few romantic notions about the place. I think of it as a place of new beginnings. Just think of all the men and women who made new beginnings, changed the very course of their lives, as a result of their having traveled to California in '49 and the years immediately following that momentous year."

"Violet isn't the only one with romantic notions," Endicott volunteered. "I have one or two of my own."

Violet smiled at him and then told Sutton, "Aaron has suggested that we travel south. Southeast, actually."

"To Texas," Endicott amended.

"Aaron tells me," Violet said, "that he thinks he might enjoy working on a ranch in Texas."

"He could do a lot worse sort of work," Sutton said. "But cowboying can be back-busting work."

"If logging hasn't broken my back by now," Endicott said with a smile, "I do strongly doubt that cowboying would accomplish that unpleasant-to-contemplate task."

"You don't plan on sticking to accounting, the job you were trained for?" Sutton asked him.

Endicott shook his head. "At this point in my life, I think of accounting as something to fall back on if necessary. But I would prefer to work with my hands out in the open."

"What about you, Luke?" Violet inquired. "Will you be returning to Virginia City now that you've done what you set out to do for me?"

"I reckon I will."

"We both thank you for everything you've done for us, Luke," Endicott said with evident sincerity and shook hands with Sutton.

Violet offered Sutton her hand.

He took it, raised it, and brushed it with his lips. He turned to leave, but at the door he halted and turned back. "Been meaning to ask you," he said, addressing Violet. "Did you have any more trouble with Dade Talbot after I left Virginia City?"

"None. I suspect, Luke, that your encounter with him— the warning you told me you gave him—was quite enough to send him packing for good."

"I wish you both the best," Sutton said and left the room.

Once downstairs in the lobby, he rented a room of his

own which turned out to be directly across the hall from Endicott's. Later, when he was alone in it, he lay down on his back on the bed it contained and stared at the ceiling, his hands clasped behind his head.

So that's that, he thought. The hunt for Endicott ended faster than I figured it would. Well, this time out sure was easier than all the time I spent traipsing around Arizona with Indians and army troopers on my tail while I was trying to find that fellow Vernon Adams that the Apaches took. Or the years I spent trailing the four bastards who murdered my brother all that long time ago.

He sighed. Yawned. Closed his eyes.

And slipped into a deep sleep during which he dreamed of finding not Aaron Endicott, not Vernon Adams, and not any more murderers but his own heart's desire which, in his turbulent dream, as in his equally turbulent waking life, continued to elude him as he tried and failed to put a name to it.

Sutton awoke to a world made bright by the sunlight that was flowing through the window of his hotel room. He lay there, squinting and stretching, and wondering sleepily where he was.

Bailey. The name of the town drifted through his mind. It was trailed by other names: Violet, Endicott.

End of the trail, he thought. It's time for me to begin backtrailing.

A faint smile appeared on his face as he thought of Cassandra Pritchett. He would have to do some sweet-talking when he got back to Virginia City to banish from Cassandra's mind any memory of Violet Wilson. The words and phrases he would speak flickered through his mind as he swung his bare legs over the side of the bed and got up.

He poured water from the pitcher on the maple bureau

into the basin sitting beside it and proceeded to wash himself. Then, whistling, he began to dress.

A door slammed as he strapped his cartridge belt around his hips. When he opened the door of his room a moment later, he heard a heavy thud immediately followed by a series of breathless grunts which, he quickly realized, were coming from behind the closed door of Endicott's room directly across the narrow hall from where he stood.

He went to the door and knocked on it. "Endicott? You all right?"

Another thud.

Sutton reached for the doorknob. Before his hand could close on it, the door flew open, striking him and knocking him backward. He collided with the wall behind him and fought to maintain his footing. As he did so, a man bounded out into the dim, windowless hall, and before Sutton could recover enough to defend himself, the man first kicked him in the small of the back and then swung a roundhouse right that landed on the back of Sutton's neck and sent him staggering to one side and then to his knees. Behind him, the man raised his two fists and brought them both down on the back of Sutton's skull.

Stunned, his vision blurring, Sutton lost his stetson and fell forward. Supporting himself on his hands and knees, his head hanging down, he was only vaguely aware of footsteps pounding up the stairs to the third floor. He put out one hand which he braced against the wall. He retrieved his hat and then got shakily to his feet, aware as he did so of the staring people who were standing shocked and speechless in the open doorways of their rooms.

He leaned back against the wall for the moment, breathing raggedly while he waited for the red and white lights that were flashing like blinding beacons in front of his eyes to stop. When they were gone a moment later, he

put on his hat and made his way to the open door of
Endicott's room. As he stepped over the room's thresh-
hold, he saw Endicott.

Lying on the floor with one hand clutching the bed's
brass headboard, Endicott was trying unsuccessfully to
get to his feet. His hair was disheveled. Blood seeped from
his nose. He blinked blearily up at Sutton.

"What happened?"

Endicott pointed with the index finger of his free hand
at the door. "Luke—get him."

"Get who?" Sutton went to Endicott and helped him up
to sit on the edge of the bed.

Endicott opened his mouth to speak but no words
came. He swallowed hard and then pointed again at the
open door where a number of curious men had gathered.

"Take it easy and tell me what happened here," Sutton
said as he continued to support Endicott who seemed
about to fall.

"He—there was a knock on the door. I got up and let
him in. He hit me. He said he was going to kill her."
Endicott seized Sutton's forearm. Gripping it tightly, he
muttered, "It was Talbot and he's gone after Violet!"

Sutton let go of Endicott. "Where's her room at?"

"Number eleven—on the third floor."

Sutton turned and sprinted from the room. In his hurry,
he knocked down one of the men who stood gaping in
Endicott's doorway. Out in the hall, he ran for the stairs
and started up them. On the floor above him, he could
hear someone shouting words he could not make out.
When he reached the landing, he saw Dade Talbot at the
far end of the hall standing in front of the closed door of
room number eleven. Talbot was wearing a gray three-
piece sack suit and a tan derby. He continued shouting
incoherently and then began pounding on the door with
both fists.

Sutton drew his gun and shouted Talbot's name.

Talbot turned as Sutton's thumb eared back the hammer of his .45. Talbot let out a wordless roar and lunged at Sutton. With one swift swing of his right arm, he knocked the gun from Sutton's hand. With his left, he plunged a powerhouse left into Sutton's gut.

Sutton fought back, his fists ricocheting off the man's jaw and rib cage.

Talbot hit him again, this time below the belt. "I'm going to kill her with my bare hands," Talbot bellowed.

Sutton stopped the man's relentless advance with a well-placed right uppercut. Talbot's face tensed. His eyes flashed fire. A rumbling began deep in his throat and quickly grew into a roar that degenerated into what seemed to Sutton to be a demented scream. The scream and Talbot's burning eyes made Sutton think of madness.

Then, after deflecting two blows Sutton threw at him, Talbot succeeded in grasping Sutton around the waist, thus pinioning both of his arms. He picked Sutton up, carried him a few steps, and then hurled him into the stairwell.

Sutton made a grab for the banister as he hit the steps and his spine felt as if it were about to snap. But he missed it and went bouncing down the steps, his teeth clacking against one another, his body silently screaming its protest against the seemingly omnipresent pain the fall was inflicting upon it. Moments later he hit the second-floor landing and for a moment just lay where he was, his world a red pit of agony in which, thanks to Dade Talbot, he had been trapped.

He had to move, had to act. He knew it. He tried to stand up—and fell down. An unknown man came to his aid and helped him to his feet. He stood there, the anonymous good samaritan supporting him, and then he shook himself free of the man and stumbled forward. He almost fell, but at the last minute, just before he was about to go down again, he reached out with both hands and managed to seize the banister at the foot of the stairs. He held tightly to it, gritting his teeth, trying not to let himself be defeated by the agony that was gnawing at him with its many savage teeth.

The sound of shattering wood above him banished the gray cloud that was steadily darkening as it began to settle on him and threatening to cause him to lose consciousness. Making a supreme effort of will, he began to haul himself hand over hand up the steps with the help of the banister. It seemed to him to take an eternity, but he finally reached the third-floor landing for the second time in what was in reality only minutes.

"Talbot!" he yelled as he saw the splintered wood of the door of room number eleven.

Talbot continued pounding on the partially shattered door and then reached through a panel he had broken to unlock the door from the inside.

Sutton staggered down the hall toward him.

Inside the room, Violet screamed.

Sutton quickened his pace, searching for his gun which Talbot had knocked out of his hand during their earlier encounter and finding no sign of it anywhere.

Talbot turned to face him and Sutton saw, with a chilling sensation that froze for a moment both his body and his mind, his own gun in Talbot's right hand. He threw himself to one side as Talbot fired and the bullet buried itself in the wall behind Sutton.

He ran forward as Talbot threw open the broken door and disappeared inside Violet's room. When he reached her open door, he saw where she stood cowering in a corner of the room, her hands covering her mouth, her eyes alive with terror as she confronted her would-be assailant.

Sutton stared in a paralyzing blend of shock and horror as Talbot fired a second time and Violet, hit, slumped moaning to the floor of her room.

SEVEN

Talbot giggled.

Sutton's glance shifted from the no longer moaning Violet who now lay motionless on the floor, one arm thrown out, the other buried beneath her body, to his own gun in Talbot's hand and then up to the man's face which wore a relaxed, almost giddy expression as he returned Sutton's shocked stare.

"Damn you, Dade Talbot!"

Endicott, who had shouted the words, appeared to stand shuddering beside Sutton. His eyes were wide, his lips quivering as he stared at Violet and the blood that was soaking through her blue nightgown. He sobbed.

Sutton, as Talbot raised the Remington in his hand, stepped in front of Endicott. When Endicott tried to move around him, he blocked the man's passage with an outstretched arm.

"I could take the two of you with one shot," Talbot said menacingly. "It would go right through you, Sutton, and into Endicott. Are you two boys ready?"

Sutton didn't know if Talbot was bluffing and he wasn't willing to wait to find out. He threw himself backward an instant after he had seized the porcelain pitcher that sat on the table to his right. He knocked Endicott and the table over and fell heavily on top of the man only a moment after he had hurled the pitcher and two shots had roared in the small room.

Then he was scrambling to his feet and picking up the

table on which the now shattered pitcher had stood. Across the room from him, Talbot lay on the floor, momentarily stunned as a result of having been hit on the forehead by the pitcher Sutton had thrown at him. Sutton took a step toward Talbot, raised the table, and brought it down.

Talbot, having seen the heavy wooden missile coming, managed to roll to one side. The table glanced off his hunched shoulders but missed his head which he had shielded with one hand.

Sutton reached down and tore his gun from Talbot's hand. As he did so, Talbot kicked out with both feet. His feet slammed against Sutton's left shin, almost snapping the bone. Sutton, temporarily crippled by the savage attack, stumbled and then almost fell as his left leg threatened to give way under him.

Talbot sprang to his feet and picked up the chair.

Sutton was unaware of the fact that Talbot was raising the chair preparatory to hitting him with it because Talbot was out of his line of vision. He jerked upright as Violet who was still lying on the floor near his feet suddenly cried, "Look out, Luke!"

He ducked as Talbot brought the table down and it crashed harmlessly against the floor, two of its legs breaking upon impact.

Talbot dropped the table and made a grab for Sutton's gun. But before he could touch it, Endicott ripped the gun from Sutton's hand.

Talbot lunged forward, both arms thrust out in front of him, and shoved Sutton into Endicott. The gun in Endicott's hand went off but no one was hit. Before Endicott could fire a second time, Talbot turned and threw himself through the closed window, shattering both its glass and frame.

Endicott ran to the broken window and stood there looking out and cursing loudly.

Sutton dragged himself across the floor to where Violet lay, her eyes half closed.

Endicott turned away from the window, placed Sutton's revolver on the bureau, and hurried back to where Violet was lying with her head in Sutton's lap as he sat on the floor beside her. Endicott dropped to his knees and took her hand which he pressed to his lips.

"I thought Talbot had killed you," he whispered in a stricken voice. "I thought you were dead." His eyes dropped to the blood that was seeping through the bodice of Violet's blue nightgown.

"I must have fainted when I was shot," she murmured.

"Go see if you can find a doctor," Sutton ordered Endicott.

A moment after Endicott had left the room, the desk clerk appeared in the doorway. "I say," the man ventured, "what seems to be the trouble here?"

Sutton, getting to his feet, answered, "It's nothing you need to fret about." He eased the clerk out of the room, closing the broken door behind him. Then he made his way back to where Violet was lying on the floor.

He picked her up and carried her over to the bed. He gently placed her on it and adjusted the pillows in order to make her as comfortable as possible. "I know you're hurting real bad," he said to her as he sat down on the bed beside her. "But Endicott's gone to get a doctor. Pretty soon you'll be fine. Just try hard to hold on till then. Do you reckon you can do that?"

Violet nodded.

"Good girl."

"Dade followed me here," she whispered.

"Maybe you'd better not talk now. Maybe—"

"He told me he followed you after you ran into him at

my house in Virginia City. That's how he found out that I was staying with Adele Fenton. He said he kept watch on me and when I—" Violet coughed.

Sutton raised the pillows and then lifted her so that her back was against them.

Her coughing subsided and she continued, "He followed me when I left town after I got your letter about Aaron, Luke. His horse went lame the second day on the trail, he said, so he lost track of me for a while. But then he picked up my trail again and followed me here to Bailey."

Violet's coughing began again. When it ended, she sat up and added in a much weaker voice, "He said he intended to strangle me. Luke, I think he's crazed. His eyes—"

As Violet sank wearily back on her pillows, Sutton, remembering Talbot's eyes and the man's wild demeanor, thought: she's right. Talbot's gone round the bend.

"When he first came here tonight," Violet said, "Dade told me he intended to kill me. He said I was unfaithful to him. He called me names—terrible names. He seemed to think we were betrothed. I couldn't reason with him though I tried desperately to do so. He swore that he would see me in my grave before he let another man have me or let me—"

Sutton waited for her to go on.

Blushing, she whispered faintly, "—or let me persist in what he called 'my whorish ways' " She looked up at Luke Sutton. "Dade is mad, Luke. I'm sure of it." She paused and glanced fearfully at the broken window where a few shards of glass still clung to what was left of its frame. Then, looking back at Sutton, she asked, "Do you think Dade will come back?"

Talbot took the trouble to trail you all the way here from Virginia City, he thought, on account of he wants you dead. So it don't strike me as anywhere near likely he'll rest till he does what he means to do, which is kill you. He said, "You rest. The doctor'll be here any minute." He could tell by the fearful look Violet gave him that she not only knew he had avoided giving her a direct answer to her question but also that she knew the ugly answer to her question without his having to tell her what he believed.

Violet closed her eyes. They opened when Sutton got up and went to the bureau to retrieve his .45 which Endicott had placed there.

"Luke?"

"I'm here."

"Why, Luke?"

Sutton returned and sat down on the edge of the bed after thumbing fresh cartridges from his belt and inserting them into the empty chambers of his gun and then holstering the weapon. "Why what?"

"Why is Dade behaving like this? I never made any kind of commitment to him. I never led him on—never lied to him. What makes him act so hateful toward Aaron and me?"

"From what I've seen, it appears that Talbot's a drinking man. Maybe the red-eye's burned out his brain."

"I think it's more than the whiskey. Dade drank—sometimes to excess—when I first knew him. But he was not then a violent or a dangerous man. Now I think he is both. As I said before, I think his obsession with me has somehow warped his thinking. I believe—"

Violet was prevented from completing her thought by the appearance of Endicott and another man whom Endicott introduced as Doctor Lane.

Sutton and Endicott left the room at the doctor's request and stood outside in the hall. Neither of them spoke as Endicott paced and Sutton leaned back against the wall.

Endicott suddenly stopped pacing. With his fists clenched tightly at his sides, he turned to Sutton and announced, "I'm going to kill Talbot."

Sutton had been expecting something of the sort. "You try something like that and you might get killed yourself."

"I can take care of myself."

"So can Talbot take care of himself or so it appears to me."

"Well, I can't go on living like this," Endicott said, seeming to argue the issue with himself rather than with Sutton. "Neither can Violet. We could be killed, both of us. I've got to take a stand. I'm through running and I damn well won't see the woman I love shot down in cold blood by a crazy man."

"You think Talbot's crazy, do you?"

"Don't you?"

Sutton said nothing.

"You saw the way he acted. But you didn't hear the things he said to me when he practically broke into my room tonight. He was raving. His eyes seemed about to pop out of his head. I tell you—and it's true—he was frothing at the mouth. Spittle ran down his chin as he denounced both Violet and myself. He claimed she had betrayed him. He said she had promised to marry him. She never did, Sutton. The man's mind is going—or is gone."

"You say you think Talbot's loco."

"That is my considered opinion based on what has happened here tonight. Not to mention his aberrant earlier behavior where both Violet and myself were concerned."

"Well, I've heard it said that only a fool or a cow camp cook would go up against a madman and you're not neither one of those."

"But I have to do something!" Endicott argued. "I—"

"Mr. Endicott."

Endicott turned to face a somber Doctor Lane who was standing in the doorway and beckoning to him.

"You can go in to her now," the doctor said.

"Is she—will she be all right?" Endicott asked anxiously.

"She's doing as well as can be expected under the circumstances, which is to say that she is weak—partly from shock and partly from a loss of blood. The bullet which struck her grazed her ribs but did not lodge in her body."

"Thank you, doctor," Endicott said and then paid the man before entering Violet's room, followed by Sutton.

Endicott hurried over to the bed, bent down, and silently embraced Violet. Then, straightening, he said, "The doctor said you'll be fine. Oh, Violet, I blame myself for what happened to you."

"Don't, Aaron. It wasn't your fault. Let's forget about the matter."

Endicott shook his head. "No," he said sternly. "I won't —can't—forget about it. In fact, I was just telling Luke before the doctor joined us that I intend to go after Talbot. When I find him, I'm going to kill him."

Violet's eyes darkened.

To Sutton, she seemed to have grown paler than she was a moment ago. He watched her reach out and take Endicott's hand in her own.

"No, Aaron," she said softly. "You mustn't think about such a thing. You've seen what Dade Talbot is capable of —to what lengths he is willing to go to hurt us. The man is not rational, I am convinced. He would, were you to go stalking him, kill you without giving the matter so much as a second thought."

"I don't want to upset you, darling," Endicott persisted, "but we have to face the facts and the facts—one of them at least, as I see it—is that Talbot might very well try again to do what he did here tonight. The only way to insure your safety in light of that fact is to eliminate Talbot. I intend to do just that."

"I understand how you feel," Violet said as she continued to hold Endicott's hand. "But look at it this way—my way. If anything happened to you—Aaron, I can tell you honestly, in that event I wouldn't want to go on living without you."

Endicott dropped to his knees beside the bed and wordlessly embraced Violet a second time. "You and I will never be safe," he whispered to her, "as long as Talbot is alive. So the path ahead is clear to me and I shall follow it."

Sutton said, "I mean to see to it that Talbot does no harm to either one of you."

Endicott turned to face him. "This is no longer your affair, Luke."

"Violet hired me to find and protect you."

"You've done your job—you've found me," Endicott pointed out somewhat harshly.

"I've done part of what I was hired to do—the finding part. I figure I've still got some of the protecting part to do."

Endicott turned his gaze on Violet. As she continued staring at Sutton, he gave her a reassuring nod.

"Luke's right," she promptly declared, evidently responding to Sutton's secret signal and deciding to play the game his way, which is what he had hoped she would do. "Let Luke deal with Dade, Aaron, in whatever way he sees fit."

"I'm willing to compromise," Endicott offered after a moment of silence. "Luke and I will try to track him down together." He looked at Violet, obviously seeking her approval of his proposal.

Unseen by Endicott, Sutton caught her eye and shook his head.

Violet turned her attention to Endicott, saying, "You

must do what you think you have to do, Aaron. I don't want to stand in your way. Or have you think me meddlesome. But—"

"Yes, darling?"

"Before you leave—do you think you could find someone to look after me for a few days, since the doctor has told me I must remain in bed for at least that long or until I fully recover? Maybe he knows someone who could look after me while you're gone."

Endicott looked at Sutton and then back at Violet. "Perhaps it would be best if I stayed with you. I don't know that there is anyone else available who could take care of you. I'm afraid I haven't been thinking clearly. I should have realized that you can't be left alone here under the circumstances."

Sutton felt like applauding Violet for the subtle way in which she had managed to maneuver Endicott into a position from which he could not escape without seeming to disregard her very real needs in favor of his passion for revenge.

"You'd do well to stay here, Endicott," Sutton advised him. "Like Violet said, she's in need of some looking after. While you're looking after her, I'll be out looking for Talbot."

Sutton paused and then continued, "I don't mean to alarm you but I think you'd do well, Endicott, to keep both your eyes open just in case Talbot should take a notion to try again to raise Cain."

"I'll do that," Endicott assured Sutton as he put a protective arm around Violet.

"What do you intend to do if and when you find Dade?" Violet asked hesitantly.

"That all depends on what he decides to do once I catch up with him," Sutton answered firmly.

Sutton was hailed by the desk clerk as he made his way through the hotel lobby. He turned and gave the man an innocent smile, saying, "The excitement's all over and done with. Nothing to worry about now." He started for the door.

The desk clerk scurried out from behind his desk and caught up with Sutton, effectively blocking his path. "I heard shots fired," the man said. "Then this man jumped down from the overhang out front. That's when I went up to inquire about the commotion. What happened up there?"

"Lover's quarrel," Sutton answered and thought that his reply, although not the whole truth by any means, was not a complete lie either. "Tell me something. Where did that fellow go once he jumped down from the overhang out front?"

"Down the street. That way." The desk clerk pointed to the west. "He must have hurt his leg because he was limping pretty bad."

"What's down that way besides the livery?" Sutton asked, pointing west as the desk clerk had just done.

"A few residences. The meeting hall. At the end of the street there's a picnic grove."

Sutton stepped around the desk clerk and left the hotel. He made his way directly to the livery. Once there, he asked the mostly elderly men who were seated on packing crates in front of the building how the livery business had been that morning.

"Slow," answered one of the men after spitting a brown stream of tobacco juice into the dust at his feet. "They's only been one customer in the past hour and a half. No, two."

Sutton described Dade Talbot and asked, "Was he one of the two?"

"Uh—yup. He come to collect his horse."

"I'm obliged to you." Sutton entered the livery and asked the stable boy he found inside what, if any thing, Talbot had said to him.

"Nothing at all, sir," the boy replied. "He wasn't one for talking much. He just paid me what he owed and took his horse and went."

"What kind of a horse was it?"

"Small buckskin. Thirteen or so hands high."

"Did you happen to see which way he went when he left here?"

"No, sir, I was too busy inside here to notice."

"I'll take my dun now," Sutton said. "How much do I owe you?"

"Is he a friend of yours by any chance, the man aboard the buckskin?" the boy asked as Sutton paid him and proceeded to saddle his horse.

"How come you ask?"

"Well, I thought that if you're fixing to join up with him, you could give him this. I didn't notice that he'd dropped it when he was paying me till after he'd gone."

Sutton took the brass check the boy was holding out to him. Compliments of Sweet Alice read the letters that were engraved on the check that served as legal tender in most Western towns. He turned it over and read the address engraved on the check's other side: 10 Brimstone Street, Helltown.

"How do you know the man I asked you about was the one who dropped this?" he asked the stable boy.

"Well, sir, I admit I didn't see him drop it with my own two eyes but I figured it must have been him as did on account of how the other customer I had so far this morning was the circuit preacher, Reverend Edwards, and I don't think he dropped it being that the only times he ever drops his pants is when he has to answer nature's calls.

"Besides which the Reverend Edwards, he's a teetotaler and the man who was passing these checks out was doing it in the saloon last night. So the Reverend couldn't have been on the receiving end since he won't so much as set foot in what I've heard him call 'Satan's swill shop.'"

"Do you happen to know where this here Helltown's located?"

After the boy had told him and he had pocketed the brass check that Talbot had apparently dropped, Sutton led his dun out of the livery and into the bright sunshine.

He swung into the saddle and headed west, leaving Bailey behind him as he moved deeper into the mountains.

He rode through a narrow valley made green by a mixture of highland grasses through which a winding stream meandered. Because the slopes on either side of him were relatively steep, he kept close to the bank of the stream, sometimes even walking his dun through its clear waters.

A bee fly buzzed persistently around his head for a time but he finally succeeded in brushing it away. When he neared the waterfall that was the source of the valley's stream—as well as several others which wandered off in different directions—he skirted it and rode into the relative darkness of a white pine forest.

Doubts assailed him as he continued his journey. Was he heading in the right direction? He had seen no sign of Talbot, so there was no way of knowing for sure whether he was or not. He wondered if he should have stayed in Bailey. What would happen if he was wrong about what Talbot had done after leaving the livery? What if Talbot had remained in town, intending to try again to murder Violet?

His hand tightened on his reins and his dun, feeling the tug on them that Sutton was not even aware he had made, slowed its pace.

Maybe, he mused, Sweet Alice's brass check hadn't been dropped by Talbot as the stable boy believed. But even if Talbot had dropped it, its mere presence in Talbot's pocket didn't guarantee that the man planned to head for Helltown to, perhaps, pay a visit to the woman whose name and address appeared on it.

Sutton heeled his dun and the horse moved out.

When he had gone another mile, he drew rein, still not sure whether he should go on or not. He sat his saddle, considering the matter. Maybe he should simply return to Virginia City. He had fulfilled his obligations to Violet Wilson and Aaron Endicott, hadn't he? He more or less had, he decided, despite what he had told Endicott earlier. But he still felt that the matter remained unfinished. His feeling had something to do with Talbot, he realized. He wanted to square things with Talbot once and for all because, he felt, the man had challenged him when he had invaded the hotel in Bailey and attempted to kill Violet. Although she had not hired him to protect her, Sutton still felt he owed her something.

He heeled his horse and moved out again. Later, as the sun was passing its meridian, he rode into Helltown. The place was not so much a town as it was a cluster of board and tarpaper shacks, some of which looked as if they were about to fall down in the face of the next wind, however light that wind might be. They bordered a rutted path that served as the town's only street. As Sutton rode down it, he headed for the only halfway solid structure within sight. A piece of wood hung above its door, nailed there at an odd angle, on which someone had burned the single word: Saloon.

He got out of the saddle, wrapped his reins around a branch of a bramble bush, and with his hand resting lightly on the butt of his revolver, stepped up to the open door of the saloon and peered inside.

The place was empty except for the bar dog who was standing behind a plank bar that rested on two barrels and a cigar-smoking man wearing a canvas duster and a round straw hat that sported a bright red band. The floor of the saloon was of dirt and decidedly uneven. On one wall someone had nailed a picture torn from a mail-order catalog which showed a woman with a beehive hairdo who was wearing only high-button shoes and a tightly laced corset.

Sutton saw no sign of Talbot. Dropping his hand from his gun, he entered the saloon. At the bar, he ordered whiskey. When it was served to him in a dirty glass, he took a sip and almost gagged.

"You got anything better than this here rotgut?" he asked the bar dog who simply shrugged and told him he was drinking the best the local still could produce. He shoved the glass to one side, leaned on the bar, and beckoned to the bar dog.

When the man leaned over toward him, he said, "I'm looking for a fellow name of Dade Talbot." He described Talbot to the bar dog. "You seen him in here lately by any chance?"

"Maybe I have and then again maybe I haven't."

"Just what might you mean by that?"

"Just that lots of the fellas who come in here have black hair—"

"Black *curly* hair I said."

"Lots of 'em have black *curly* hair and are built blocky like you said the man you're looking for is. Lots of them have pointy chins and thick lips too."

"Where's number ten Brimstone Street?"

"The street out front—that's Brimstone Street. It's also the only street we got." The bar dog grinned.

Sutton didn't. He repeated his question.

"Number ten's two doors down—it's the shack with the paper rose tacked to its door."

Sutton turned, and leaving his drink on the bar, left the saloon. When he reached number ten Brimstone Street, he knocked on the door that was adorned with a faded pink paper rose.

"Go away!" a woman's voice called out from behind the closed door. "I'm busy."

"I've come a long way to see you if your name's Sweet Alice."

A moment later, a woman opened the door.

"My, but aren't you the good-looking fellow?" she cooed, pulling up the bodice of her dress with one hand and brushing back a strand of brown hair that had fallen over her forehead with the other.

Sutton took the brass check from his pocket and held it up. *"Are* you Sweet Alice?"

"It pays to advertise," the woman said. Then, leaning around the door frame, she whispered, "I just got started with my current client. Come back in ten minutes."

"I just want to ask you a question or two. I—"

"You don't want to—you know?" Sweet Alice frowned at Sutton, perplexed—or, possibly, disappointed.

"Not this time," he told her.

"Mister, I run a business. I don't have time to waste answering stranger's questions. Time is money. At least, *my* time is." She slammed the door in Sutton's face.

He raised his fist to knock on it again and then thought better of it, deciding instead to wait until Sweet Alice's business transaction that was taking place inside the shack was completed. Then he would try once again to have a talk with her.

Less than ten minutes later, the door opened again and a somewhat disheveled Sweet Alice stood there, her eyes on Sutton, a lustful look in them.

"You wanted to talk to me?" she prompted and Sutton responded with, "I very much do."

"Come on in then and let's"—she gave Sutton a teasing smile—"talk."

He followed her into the one-room shack, and when he saw that it was empty of any other person, asked, "I thought you had a customer in here with you."

"I did," Sweet Alice said laconically. "He's gone—out the back door." She came up to Sutton and put her arms around his neck. "Now what was it you wanted to talk to Sweet Alice about?"

Sutton was about to speak when she suddenly put a finger to his lips and said, "I must mind my manners. We'll have a little drink first." She left him, took a bottle of whiskey out of a cupboard along with two glasses, and with her back to him, poured two drinks, one of which she handed to Sutton.

"I was in the saloon just before I came here," he told her, "and I found the local red-eye hard to swallow. So if you won't take offense, I'll pass on this for now."

"This whiskey didn't come from the local still," Sweet Alice told him. "One of my gentlemen callers made me a present of this." She raised her glass and touched it with a faint *chink* to Sutton's. "Here's looking at you."

She drank and so did Sutton after which he asked her if she had seen Talbot whom he described to her in detail.

She frowned, furrowing her forehead. Then, with an index finger tapping her chin, she seemed to ponder the question. After a moment, "I see so many men in my line of work. After a while, they all begin to blur in my memory. I can't remember most of them and those I can remember—well, let me put it this way. It's not always their faces I remember." Laughter, shrill and raucous, spilled from between her lips for a moment. Then she emptied her glass, urged Sutton to do the same, and when he had also emptied his glass, she took it from him and refilled it.

"Happy days," she toasted.

They drank.

Sutton asked her to try hard to remember whether she had seen Talbot recently. "He had your brass check in his pocket I'm told, so I figured there was a good chance he might be heading your way."

Something's wrong, he thought. What? He wasn't sure. And then, when he asked Sweet Alice if she had heard his question, he knew what was wrong. His speech had become slurred.

He looked down at the half-empty glass in his hand. The whiskey? Was it that powerful?

He looked from the glass in his hand to Sweet Alice who was standing with her arms folded in front of him while she watched him closely. She seemed to shift from side to side as he watched her and yet he could have sworn she hadn't moved a muscle. A moment later he saw three of her.

"Something wrong?" he heard her ask him as if she were speaking to him from a great distance.

wrong, wrong, wrong . . .

The word echoed in the room. It invaded Sutton's mind and boomed there, causing him to close his eyes in an attempt to ward off the sound that was accompanied by a sudden wave of giddiness that swept over him.

—sit down, down, down . . .

"Yes," he said and heard the word emerge from between his lips as *yesshhh.*

He let Sweet Alice help him to a rope bed that sat against one wall of the shack. He slumped down upon it, the glass in his hand falling to the dirt floor.

Sweet Alice disappeared. Or was she still there and he

couldn't see her because of the way his eyes were so swiftly dimming?

The whiskey, he thought. She put something in it.

He tried to rise. Couldn't. Tried to focus his eyes. Couldn't.

. . . the whiskey, he thought dreamily as he felt himself slipping into a dark world that was soft and yet somehow sinister. She drugged me, he thought just before that dark world claimed him.

EIGHT

Talbot gleefully taunted Sutton with words and gestures but Sutton, inexplicably paralyzed, could not move a muscle to attempt to apprehend his quarry.

Talbot gamboled and gyrated, chanting snatches of obscene songs and alternately daring Sutton to try to take him.

Sutton strained every muscle in his body in an attempt to move forward and put his hands on the man he had been hunting. But invisible bonds immobilized him.

A roar of frustration escaped his lips and he tried once more to move, the cords in his neck standing out, his heart pounding. . . .

He broke free of whatever had been binding him and lunged at Talbot—who disappeared into a suddenly descending darkness in which Sutton foundered alone and then . . .

Light.

It seeped from an unknown source, and all too slowly to suit the impatient Sutton, began to vanquish the blinding darkness in which he found himself.

Sutton's drugged dream gradually gave way to reality. He opened his eyes, blinked, and looked around the room he recognized as belonging to Sweet Alice. He sat up on the bed where he had been lying, and as he did so, his head began to spin. He closed his eyes and placed the palms of his hands on either side of his head. As the giddiness he had been feeling gradually dissipated, he opened his eyes and took his hands away from his head.

He swore under his breath as he thrust a hand into his pocket and found that the three dollars he had had there were gone. She stole my money, he thought, and then began to grin. He thrust a hand into his left boot and was relieved to find the second five hundred dollars Violet had paid him plus the remainder of his money which he had stored there before reaching Helltown. She missed the big bonanza he thought with satisfaction as he pocketed a few dollars and returned the rest of his poke to its hiding place.

He got unsteadily to his feet and looked around the empty room. She's flown the coop with my money he thought as he made his way outside and returned to the saloon.

The bar dog was the saloon's only occupant, and when he saw Sutton approaching him, he called out, "I wondered what had happened to you. I've got some news you might like to hear."

"First of all though I've got a question for you. Do you happen to know where Sweet Alice is?"

"On her back on her bed no doubt," sneered the bar dog.

"She's not and she's got money of mine she stole from me."

The bar dog's eyebrows arched. "Oh, ho! So she slipped you a dose of chloral, did she?"

"How do you know that?"

"I don't know it. I just guessed it. That's what she does with strangers—most of them who come to her. She don't risk it though with her regular clients. How much did she take you for?"

"Where does she go to ground at a time like this?" Sutton inquired, ignoring the question.

"Nobody knows. She disappears after she's taken a sucker—a gentleman. Sometimes for days at a time. But she'll show up again if you've got the patience to wait around awhile."

"You said when I came in here that you had some news I might like to hear. What sort of news were you talking about?"

"That fellow—that *curly-haired* fellow—you asked me about the last time you were here?"

"What about him?"

"He came in after you left."

Sutton's fingers tightened on the plank that served as a bar. "Where is he now?"

"Gone."

A feeling of disappointment that was blended with anger arose in Sutton. "Gone where?"

"West."

"What kind of horse was he riding?" Sutton asked suspiciously, wondering if the bar dog was telling him a tall tale, possibly in the hope of receiving a reward of some kind.

"A buckskin."

Sutton's suspicions subsided. He tossed a dollar on the bar. "I'm obliged to you."

Once outside again, he started for his horse. But, before he reached it, he halted, turned, and went back to the open door of the saloon where he yelled to the bar dog, "How long ago was that fellow I asked you about in here?"

"Over an hour ago," came the bar dog's answer. "When I went and told him you were looking for him—I figured you two were friends and I would be doing you both a favor by telling him you were asking after him—he got real edgy and left without even drinking his drink—or paying me for it either."

"You're sure it was the man I described to you?" Before

the bar dog could answer, Sutton proceeded to describe Talbot to him a second time, including the clothes—the tan derby and gray three-piece sack suit—the fugitive had been wearing the last time Sutton had seen him.

"It was him sure enough," the bar dog declared with certainty. "No doubt in my mind about it."

Sutton went to his horse, freed it, swung into the saddle, and rode west.

Helltown was far behind him when he spotted the rider in the distance. Or, more accurately, the dust the rider was raising in the distance. It blended with the mist that was floating through the valley Sutton found himself in as the sun disappeared below a jagged series of mountain peaks.

Sutton drew rein and sat his saddle, watching the dust. Minutes later, a rider materialized in front of it as the man came closer to where Sutton waited.

It's not Talbot, Sutton thought with a feeling of disappointment. He moved his dun out, angling it toward the rider who was north of him as the man rode east. When he came within hailing distance, he hallooed the stranger and waved a greeting. Then, when the man had brought his horse to a halt and acknowledged Sutton's greeting with a wave of his own, Sutton rode up to the man.

"I've been trying to catch up with a fellow I know," he told the man who was watching him through slightly narrowed eyes. Sutton described Talbot to him, including the three-piece suit and derby he was wearing, concluding with, "He's atop a buckskin. Have you seen him?"

"I seen him."

Sutton felt excitement surging through him. "Where? When?"

"Spotted him off to my south about an hour ago, maybe a little less. He was traveling the same trail you were following."

"I'm obliged to you for the information," Sutton told the other rider and then went galloping west in pursuit of his prey.

He reluctantly slowed his dun from a gallop to a canter as he rode into rough country that was scattered with broken fragments of boulders and pocked here and there with badger holes. He kept his eyes on the ground ahead of him as he guided his mount through the treacherous ground while simultaneously searching for sign of Talbot.

He found what he was looking for a little farther on when he came to a wide draw through which a stream flowed swiftly. On either side of the stream, the ground was swampy which, Sutton guessed, was the result of the flooding which in turn was the result of the mountain top's melting snow which had recently swollen the stream. Clearly outlined in the wet ground were the hoofprints of a horse and Sutton could readily see that the horse was no wild animal. It was shod, and judging by the depth of the tracks it had left, it was bearing weight on its back.

Talbot?

Sutton made his necessarily slow and therefore frustrating way through the draw, his dun's hooves sinking deep into the muck under them, and emerged a little more than ten minutes later on solid ground. There he was still able to make out the tracks of what he believed to be Talbot's buckskin, although they were fainter now. He rode toward the mountain slope facing him, and when he reached it, still following the plain trail he had found, he began to ascend the mountain.

His dun snorted as it struggled up the relatively steep slope in the deepening shadows. Its breath formed puffs of steam because of the chill that had swiftly iced the air following the sun's descent. Its feet scrabbled for purchase and occasionally slipped on the rock-littered ground.

Sutton, to ease the animal's valiant struggle, drew rein and got out of the saddle. Then, leading the dun, he began to scramble up the slope. The higher he went the more he had to fight for breath in the thinning air. But he did not stop to rest, unwilling as he was to lose any time, intent only on closing in on Talbot as quickly as he could.

He was still several hundred yards from the summit when a rifle shot sounded. He froze momentarily as shards of stone went flying through the air from the boulder on his left which the rifleman had hit. Then he dived behind a boulder, his head down, his legs bent beneath him.

Another shot tore through the deepening darkness and whined over his head.

Sutton looked up at the summit and saw a man up there above him, a rifle in his hands.

It's Talbot, Sutton thought with delight as he recognized Talbot's three-piece sack suit and tan derby, although he could not see Talbot's face because the light was behind the man, silhouetting him.

His hand went to the butt of his six-gun as he continued to stare up at Talbot who had brazenly—or perhaps foolishly—skylined himself. But he didn't unleather it. Talbot makes a perfect target up there, he thought. He does, that is, for somebody who has a rifle, which I don't at the moment. My sidearm can't touch him, not at this range it can't.

Then shorten the distance between us, he advised himself. You do that and you'll have a chance to even the score. Even while the thought was occurring to him, Sutton was on the move. Still gripping his dun's reins, he made himself ready, and when his attacker fired a brief volley of two more shots, both of which missed him, he made his move. He ran crouching and pulling hard on the reins toward an outcropping of rock that he had noticed earlier which would afford him better protection from his assailant than did the boulder he had been sheltering behind.

He made it safely to his chosen refuge but his dun did not. An instant before the dun would have been hidden behind the ledge, as Sutton now was, the rifleman fired again and this time he hit the horse.

The dun screamed, broke free of Sutton, and went racing down the slope to disappear among some trees.

"Damn you, Talbot!" Sutton shouted at the top of his voice. "I'm coming up there after you, and when I get there, you'll rue the devilish day you were born!"

Sutton skirted the rocky ledge, moving to the right. Where the ledge ended, he hesitated a moment and then, with his eyes on some saplings that were sprouting not far above him which would afford him some cover, he headed up the slope toward them.

He took shelter momentarily among them and then, when no more shots sounded, he left the protection of the trees and went zigzagging across an expanse of open terrain toward a gulch he had spotted some distance away. When he reached it, he leapt down into it and crouched there.

He had barely caught his breath when he turned, and taking off his hat, straightened and peered over the edge of the gulch. He saw no sign of his attacker. Maybe he's shifted position, he thought. So he can get a bead on me here where I'm at now.

Clapping his hat back on his head, he ran down the length of the gulch. At its mouth he paused, but only for a moment, before darting out of the gulch and sprinting farther up the mountain. He moved from tree to tree as he approached the summit, sometimes running at right angles to his upward path to confuse the rifleman above him, reasoning that Talbot just might be smart enough to pick out the next tree he was heading for if he made the mistake of moving in a straight line as he worked his way upward.

When he was almost at the summit, he changed tactics, deciding on a flank attack. He got down on the ground, drew his gun, and clutching it tightly in his right hand, began to crawl along the ground in a southerly direction. He went rigid as a shot was fired at him and then scrambled as fast as he could along the ground as dirt flew up only a yard away from his previous position.

When he reached the cover of some wild chokecherry, he hunkered down for a moment and then made a dash for the summit. He had just reached it when he heard a horse nicker. Turning, he peered in the direction from which the sound had come but could see little because the fast-fading light that remained, which was turning the sky above him a blood-red, could not conquer the shadows that were everywhere on the mountainside.

When he heard hoofbeats, he realized his quarry was getting away from him. Springing to his feet, he began to run in the direction of the thudding sounds. He topped the summit and gazed down the other side as he searched for sign of horse and rider. But he saw neither. He could only hear the sound of snapping limbs and the cracking of deadwood as the horse tore through a stand of sugar pine.

Sutton suppressed the urge to race after his fleeing quarry, for he knew it would do him no good to do so. You made a damned dumb mistake, he silently chastised himself, coming way the hell up here without a horse. You'll never catch up to Talbot on foot. What's more and what's worse, you'll never be able to trail him in the dark. Frustrated and angry, Sutton turned and made his way back down the mountain. When he reached the place where his horse had been shot, he began to search for the animal. It was not until the horned moon was high in the sky that he finally found the dun standing stiffly on the bank of the stream that wound its way through the draw he had been in earlier.

As he approached the animal, it drew away from him. He spoke to it softly, standing stock-still for a moment before attempting to approach it again. It blew. He took several steps toward it, still speaking to it in a voice that was little more than a whisper.

The horse swung its head toward him and snorted. As Sutton came up beside it, the animal pawed the ground with one front hoof. Its tail swished back and forth. Its ears snapped up, fell back against its head.

Sutton placed one hand on its neck and began to stroke it as he searched for the animal's wound by the light of the moon which was growing faint as the sky began to cloud over. He finally found it on the horse's opposite side. The bullet that had hit the animal had grazed its neck and singed a portion of its mane. Sutton examined the wound which, he soon discovered to his relief, was not deep. The bullet had done little damage other than leave a seared line of sundered flesh just below the dun's jaw.

"You and me," Sutton whispered to his mount, "we're going to spend the night right here where we're at." I'd have as much chance of catching a will-o'-the-wisp as I would have of catching Talbot, he thought, in a night as dark and cloudy as this.

The following morning's first light found Sutton already on Talbot's trail. He rode through a thick mist that hid the peaks above him and occupied the valley through which he was traveling.

He had picked up his quarry's plain trail easily on the far side of the slope from which Talbot had fired at him. Talbot was riding hard and apparently heedless about covering his tracks. Sutton rode into a canyon, its tall walls blocked out the sunlight. He squinted at the ground as he rode, occasionally noticing sign—a chipped rock, soft droppings—that told him he was heading in the right direction.

He had almost reached the distant mouth of the canyon where the walls of rimrock above him angled sharply down toward the level ground when he thought he heard a sound. It had been a sharp sound, something grating on something else loud enough to be heard above the sound his dun's hooves made as they struck the hardpan of the canyon floor.

The sound came again and this time Sutton recognized it as shoe leather scraping on stone and that it had come from above him. He looked up.

A man with outstretched arms came hurtling down toward him through the mist.

Before Sutton could make a defensive move, the man's body struck him, knocked him out of the saddle, and sent his dun dancing to one side. He hit the ground hard with the other man's bulky body on top of his. His breath was knocked from him by the fall. As he gasped, sucking air into his depleted lungs, his throat was seized by the man straddling him who began to squeeze.

Sutton's fingers clawed desperately at his attacker's hands but he was unable to dislodge them. Choking, he brought both knees up and slammed them into the small of the man's back, causing him to lose his grip and fly forward over Sutton's head.

Sutton rolled over, and gagging, got to his knees. As his attacker started to rise from the ground, he drew his gun. "Freeze!" he ordered.

Instead of obeying Sutton's order, the downed man dropped abruptly back on his buttocks and kicked upward with one booted foot, striking Sutton's hand and knocking the gun from it.

Both men made a grab for the weapon as it hit the

ground, but it was Sutton who succeeded in retrieving it. He brought it up and then down on his opponent's temple, knocking him to the ground where he lay silent and motionless.

With his gun in his hand, Sutton sat down on the nearby boulder not far from his dun to wait for the bushwhacker to regain consciousness.

"You want to tell me what's going on?" Sutton asked less than five minutes later as the fallen man's eyes flickered open.

"Figure it out for yourself."

"Maybe I already have," Sutton said to the man who was wearing Talbot's clothes but who, he had discovered when he got his first good look at him during the fight, was not Talbot but the lone man he had last seen sitting in the saloon in Helltown just before his visit to Sweet Alice. "Talbot switched clothes and horses with you and told you to lay down a false trail for me to follow. How much did he pay you for all that?"

The man lying on the ground sat up and said, "None of your business."

An unperturbed Sutton continued, "Talbot cooked up a story and paid the bar dog to tell it to me so I'd ride west thinking it was Talbot I was trailing. But what I can't figure out is how Talbot knew I was in Helltown. I reckon maybe you can tell me that."

When the man remained sullenly silent, Sutton sprang to his feet, seized him with his free left hand and hauled him to his feet. He slammed him back against the trunk of a tree, and placing the muzzle of his .45 against his prisoner's forehead, muttered, "If you don't talk, mister, you'll be helping to stoke the fires in Hell tonight."

"Don't shoot!" the man pleaded. "I'll tell you what you want to know."

Sutton kept his gun's muzzle pressed against the man's

forehead and repeated his question which the man quickly answered.

"Talbot told me he found out you were in Helltown when you went to Sweet Alice's place. He was already there and all set to have at Alice when you showed up. He saw you through the open door. When she told you to wait, he told her you were after him. He offered to pay her ten dollars to try to keep you at her place awhile—long enough for him to get away.

"Alice was willing. She said she'd slip you some chloral in a drink which she claimed would put you out of action for a few hours, but for that she wanted twenty dollars. Talbot gave it to her."

When the man fell silent, Sutton ordered him to go on.

"Talbot hightailed it out Alice's back door. He told me at first he intended to get his buckskin which he'd left in a shed behind the saloon and ride out of town just as fast as ever he could. But then, he said, he hatched the notion of trying to hire somebody to pretend to be him on his horse so that somebody could lead you astray and—"

"Try to kill me."

"Listen, it wasn't nothing personal. It was a business deal, pure, plain, and simple."

"Since we're on the subject of you trying to kill me, what I'm wondering is how come you didn't use your rifle on me instead of jumping me like you just did."

"My rifle jammed. I've got no other gun."

"How much did Talbot pay you to kill me or was the killing included in the overall price he paid you to keep me away from him?"

The man shook his head. "He told me if I met him later and could show him your corpse, he'd pay me a hundred dollars on top of the forty he already paid me to pretend to be him. I agreed to the deal and that's when he said we should switch clothes to confuse you into thinking I was him. Well, we did and then Talbot gave me his buckskin and I gave him my horse and I rode west while he went in the opposite direction."

"You're sure he headed east? Or are you setting me up for another wild-goose chase?"

"No, it's the truth I'm telling you. I swear it is."

"Where were you supposed to meet Talbot to show him my dead body?"

"In a logging town called Bailey. He told me he was heading there. He said he had an old score to settle there."

Sutton stepped back from his prisoner but kept his gun trained on the man. "What kind of a horse did you turn over to Talbot?"

"Mine was a wall-eyed gray."

"Where's your horse?"

"I left him up on the ridge where I was waiting for you to show up."

"Let's go get him." Sutton gestured with his gun and his prisoner turned and started for the mouth of the canyon with Sutton following close behind him.

Just as they reached the canyon entrance, the man in front of Sutton suddenly doubled over and let out a groan. Sutton halted. The man gasped. As Sutton took a step toward him to see what was the matter, the man suddenly spun around. In his hand was a .28, single-shot derringer. He thrust his arm out, his finger on the gun's trigger.

But Sutton, the instant he had seen the man's hideout gun, had fired his .45. His shot shattered his would-be killer's gun hand and then continued its deadly journey into the man's chest.

Sutton stepped back as the man went down to lie bleeding on the ground, his breath coming in short sharp gusts. His eyes stared up at Sutton in startled horror for a moment. Then he raised his wounded hand from which the thumb was missing and grimaced as he stared at it.

"You must have wanted that hundr*e*d dollars awful bad," Sutton said to him.

The man tried to speak but no words came. He looked away from Sutton as if he were trying to banish him from his world. He coughed once and then a second time. His head fell to one side as his eyes dulled in death.

Sutton calmly proceeded to fill the empty chambers of his .45. Then he made his way out of the canyon and up onto the rimrock where he found Talbot's buckskin browsing the bark of a young yellow pine.

He got a good grip on the horse's reins and led it down from the rimrock to where his dun waited inside the canyon. Without giving the man he had just killed in self-defense another look, Sutton swung into the saddle, and leading the buckskin, headed east.

Later, as he emerged from the canyon, snow began to fall and quickly covered the shriveled remains of shooting-star blossoms that lined the perimeter of a copse of willows. As the air grew chill, bringing a memory of winter in the month of July to the high country, Sutton, shivering, rode on. A mile farther on, he alarmed a fat marmot that crossed his path, causing the creature to whistle its disapproval of his intrusive presence.

The snow thickened. A wind rose, whipping playfully at first through the trees and then, as if sensing its growing strength, it began to toss snow everywhere and to cause a lacy network of frost crystals to from on the clumps of sedge that dotted the ground over which Sutton rode.

Just before noon the snowstorm stopped, leaving only a few stray flakes to drift in the air beneath a rapidly clearing sky. The last of the snowflakes melted in midair as the sun suddenly emerged from the clouds and sent its rays beaming hotly down upon the whitened mountains.

Sutton made his nooning, of necessity, in mid-afternoon because it was not until then that he came upon a sprawling growth of pigweed that covered nearly an acre of ground. He dismounted and pulled up several plants which he stored in his saddlebag. Then he pulled up others, broke off their roots, and after getting back into the saddle, began to hungrily devour the succulent stems and leaves of the plants, remembering as he did so a woman named Miranda he had once known who had somewhat fastidiously called the pigweed by its more formal name: purslane. He remembered how she had pickled the stems of the plants in a broth of white vinegar, water, salt, dill flowers, and garlic.

Those were hardscrabble times for Miranda and me, he recalled, as he continued eating his makeshift meal. We not only ate pickled pigweed, but we also ate it in soups and hotcakes and fried with a mix of eggs and bread crumbs till I began to think it would soon start oozing out my ears. He smiled as he thought of how, during that one tough summer, he and Miranda had competed with their cow for their fair share of the pigweed that grew among the sagebrush surrounding their cabin.

During the rest of that day, Sutton searched for sign of Talbot but found none, finally admitting to himself long after sundown as he was making camp for the night that he had lost the man's trail.

NINE

Sutton was still more than twenty miles from Bailey as he made his way through the mountains astride Talbot's buckskin while trailing his dun when the buckskin first faltered under him and then went down, throwing him to the ground.

He lost his grip on the dun's reins as he fell and rolled over, losing his hat as he collided with a ragged pile of limestone shale. He got to his feet, retrieved his hat, and went over to the buckskin which was lying still—too still—on its side a few feet away.

Sutton, as he clapped his hat back on his head, noted apprehensively that the animal's barrel was motionless. He hunkered down beside the horse and put his hand directly in front of its nostrils. Then he pressed the same hand against the animal's barrel. He felt no breath. No heartbeat.

I rode that horse to death, he thought. But there was just no help for it. I had to get back to Bailey in a hurry, and though I traveled as fast as I could and killed a horse doing it, I may well turn out to have traveled not near fast enough. An image of Violet Wilson flashed in his mind. It was promptly followed by a grim image of Dade Talbot.

Sutton swung into the saddle. He moved his dun out, keenly aware as he did so of the horse's labored breathing and hoping that the dun would not also give out on him.

It didn't, but by the time Sutton rode into Bailey later

that day, the dun was, as Sutton told the stableman with whom he left the animal, "on his last legs."

"Water him and see that he has enough to eat," Sutton told the liveryman. "Give him some corn if you've got it or some oats if you've not. Water and rub him down good. Check him for saddle sores and wash out my saddle blanket. I'll be back." Sutton paid the man in advance for his services and then hurriedly left the livery and made his way to the hotel, refusing to let himself give in to the fatigue that felt like an almost overwhelming dead weight bearing down upon him.

At the hotel, he asked the desk clerk if Miss Violet Wilson was still staying at the hotel. Relief flooded over him when the desk clerk told him she was. "Is she all right, do you know?"

"She is as far as I know. She had pretty much recovered, she told me yesterday, from her gunshot wound."

"She still in the same room as before?"

"Yes." As Sutton started for the steps leading to the upper floors, the desk clerk called out, "Miss Wilson is not in at the moment, sir."

Sutton returned to the desk. "Where is she?"

"I really couldn't say, sir. But you're welcome to wait for her here in the lobby, should you desire to do so."

Sutton took a seat across from the desk where he could see the hotel's front entrance. He slumped down in the soft upholstered chair he had chosen and spread his legs out in front of him. He folded his hands across his waist and let his head lean against the tall back of the chair.

"Luke."

Sutton first stirred sleepily and then awoke at the sound of his name, until then unaware that he had fallen asleep. His eyes snapped open and he found himself staring up at Violet.

"Oh, Luke," she cried, "I can't tell you how glad I was to see you here when I came in just now."

"I lost track of Talbot," Sutton told Violet as he got to his feet. "I came back here as fast as I could on account of how I heard he was on his way back here. But I take it he's not put in an appearance, since you seem to be all right."

"Luke, I'm not."

"You're not all right? What's wrong?"

"Come upstairs with me and I'll tell you."

Sutton followed Violet upstairs. When they were seated facing one another in her room, she pulled off her bonnet, tossed it on the bed, and announced, "Aaron's gone."

"Gone where?"

"After Dade."

"I thought you and me had talked him into staying put right here—at least till you got fit again and could travel with him to wherever you two decided you wanted to settle."

"I thought so too," Violet said solemnly. "And he did stay with me as he promised he would. He was the very soul of kindness. I do believe my convalescence was considerably shortened by his care and concern."

"What happened?"

"Yesterday Aaron and I were out walking after I had paid a visit to the doctor and who should we happen to see coming out of the saloon and heading for the hotel but Dade Talbot."

"So he did beat me back here after all."

"Apparently so. When he saw us, he drew the gun he was wearing and fired at us. But, in the instant before he did, Aaron managed to shove me into the space between the bank and the tin shop so I was unharmed. So, in fact, was Aaron, due I think, to Dade's bad aim. Dade was obviously intoxicated at the time. I imagine he visited the saloon upon arriving in town in order to fortify himself before coming to the hotel—to Aaron and me.

"Aaron, once he was sure that I was unhurt, told me he was going after Dade. I pleaded with him not to do so. I pointed out to him that he was unarmed but Aaron was like a man gone mad. He swore he would kill Dade—with his bare hands if he had to. There was nothing I could do or say to stop him. He made me promise to stay where I was and then he left me."

"He went after Talbot?"

Violet nodded. "I peeped around the corner of the bank and saw him take a gun from the holster of a man who happened to be passing. He fired a shot at Dade who by that time was coming toward us. He missed. People were shouting and running for cover. The man whose gun Aaron had taken was loudly and roundly condemning him as a thief in no uncertain terms. I heard another shot. I drew back. When next I dared to peep around the corner of the bank, I could see no sign of either Aaron or Dade. I waited a moment and then, breaking my promise to Aaron to stay where I was, I went in search of him."

"You didn't find him."

"No, I didn't, I'm sorry to say. Obviously, Aaron has gone after Dade and I have neither seen nor heard from him since late yesterday afternoon when all that I've just described to you took place."

Sutton got up and went to the window where he stood looking out with his hands clasped behind his back. After a moment, he remarked, "I can't say as I blame Endicott for doing what he did." He turned from the window, and in a harsher voice, added, "But I sure as hell—beg pardon, Violet—wish he'd not gone and done it."

"I share your sentiments, Luke. In fact, I'm terrified when I think that Aaron could be killed—might already have been killed because of his foolhardiness."

"What he's done, I wouldn't exactly call it foolhardy. Talbot backed him into a corner and I reckon he'd had just about all he could take. Talbot didn't leave him much of a choice. He could either turn tail and run or fight back."

"Still, I wish he had stayed here with me. We could have gone away when I was well enough." Violet, who had been studying her hands which were twisting nervously in her lap, looked up at Sutton. "You think that would be running, don't you?"

"In a way it would be. In a way it would also be the healthy thing to do. It's a whole lot healthier sometimes to pull your freight instead of your gun. But what I think about what Endicott's done don't much matter. What does matter is what's to be done now."

"I've been thinking about that ever since Aaron disappeared yesterday afternoon," Violet said. "I could, to be truthful, think of nothing else. I vowed to myself that if you came back here I would beg you to go after Aaron. I made up my mind to ask you to find him once again and persuade him to abandon the dangerous path he has chosen to travel. I can pay you, for your services, Luke. I still have some money left."

"You paid me once. Once is enough."

"But I didn't pay you to find Aaron a second time, Luke, and I don't want to take advantage of you. I want to be fair."

As Violet rose and took some bills from her reticule which had been resting on top of the bureau, Sutton shook his head.

Violet studied his face and then replaced the bills. "Thank you, Luke," she said simply and sat down again. Drawing a breath, she continued, "Since Aaron left, I made up my mind to one thing."

"What's that?"

"Let me answer you in this fashion, Luke. I not only want you to find Aaron but I also want you to find Dade."

Sutton hesitated a moment and then, "I can understand you wanting me to round up Endicott but how come you want me to run down Talbot too?"

"When you find him—Dade, I mean—tell him I will accede to his demands if he will promise not to harm Aaron."

Sutton stared silently at Violet.

Squaring her shoulders, she went on, "I'm sure you disapprove of my decision, Luke. But I can see no other way out of this conundrum. So I made up my mind to give in to Dade's demands. Only in that way can this matter be ended once and for all.

"Find Aaron for me, Luke. Tell him I am sorry but this is the way things must be from now on in order to insure his safety as well as my own. Otherwise, Dade might kill one or both of us. There is just no way that I can see to outwit him. I am convinced now that he will follow us for the rest of our lives—and when he finds us the next time . . ."

"I'm sorry, Violet."

"Sorry?"

"Yep. On two scores. One that you've decided to do what you just told me you want to do and two that I wasn't able to help you find a happier way out of this box Talbot's got both you and Endicott in."

"None of this is your fault, Luke. You did what I asked you to do. If it's anyone's fault, it's mine—mine and Aaron's."

"I can't see that."

"What I mean is that Aaron and I should have gone away right after we were reunited here in Bailey. If we had done that, Dade would not have found us and shot me." Violet slowly shook her head. "No, I'm afraid that wouldn't have solved the problem either. If we had gone away then, Aaron and I, Dade would simply have continued to follow us."

"You know what you're doing, don't you? You're doing the same thing Endicott did back in Virginia City when he wrote you that letter and then left town. Now here you are telling me to find Endicott and then Talbot and tell them both you're hooking up with Talbot. It amounts to pretty much the same thing, as I see it, that Endicott did to try to protect you."

Violet sighed wearily, her eyes lowered, "I suppose you're right. I suppose I am something of a quitter." When she looked up at Sutton again, her eyes were fiery. "But I've made up my mind. I'm going to do it—with your help. It's the only way to end this madness. It's the only sure way to keep Aaron from being killed by Dade who, I'm now convinced, will kill him if he ever gets the chance. He tried to kill Aaron yesterday. He no longer threatens only me but Aaron as well now. I just hope I'm not too late in reaching my decision—for Aaron's sake. Luke, will you help me?"

"I try hard not to leave unfinished any job I start. So, yes, I'll go see if I can't turn up Endicott and Talbot too and tell them both what you just told me."

"Oh, Luke," Violet cried, rising and taking his hand in both of hers, "I knew I could count on you."

To help you step into a trap, he thought, that's going to bring you some shame as well as a whole lot of pain, it seems to me. But the decision's not mine to make about what she's to do with her life, he told himself. Neither is it up to me to remark on what wild things a man like Endicott or a woman like Violet here'll go and do for love. But what I can do is see that she's safe till I get back—at least as safe as I can arrange for her to be.

"I don't think it's a good idea for you to stay on here," he told her. "Talbot might show up again, and if he does, there's bound to be trouble. This here's the first place he'll come looking for you if he does show up."

"You want me to change my room?"

Sutton shook his head. "I think you'd best get out of Bailey altogether."

"But where in the world could I go?"

During the time they had been talking, Sutton had asked himself the same question when he first conceived the idea of taking Violet to a place where Talbot might not be able to find her. The answer he had come up with was the one he now gave her. "There's a logging camp a few miles from here where Endicott and I worked for a time. It's far from fancy but maybe you won't have to stay there long. Get your things together and I'll take you there."

Later that day Sutton, with Violet seated beside him in the buggy he had rented at the livery in Bailey, rode into the logging camp and headed directly for the building that was the domain of the cook named Landers.

Once there, he halted the team and then helped Violet down from the buggy. Together they entered the building, the air of which was aromatic with the smells of cooking. They made their way through a maze of plank tables and benches toward the door at the rear of the room through which tendrils of steam drifted.

They found Landers in the kitchen beyond the door, industriously stirring the contents of a huge iron pot.

"Well, so you're back," Landers greeted Sutton. "You sure do come and go a lot. What's your name—no, don't tell me. My memory's still good. It's Samson. No—Sutton."

"You got it, Landers. And this here's Miss Violet Wilson. She's in need of a place to stay for a time and I thought you might be able to help her out. If you can't, I'll go talk to the bull of the woods and see what he might be able to do for us."

"Don't you make a move," Landers admonished, waving the dripping wooden spoon with which he had been stirring the contents of the pot at Sutton and Violet. "I could put you up, Miss Wilson, in my own room. It's just back there beyond the kitchen. It's rough digs but I can tidy it up some before you settle in."

"I'm sure the room you speak of will suit me, Mr. Landers," Violet said, "and of course I'll be happy to pay you for the use of it, but I do feel guilty about putting you out."

"I can bed down out here," Landers told her. "You won't be putting me out one bit. Why, it'll be a pure pleasure to be able to lay eyes on such a pretty lady like you in the days to come instead of having to all the time see nothing but rough-and-tumble timber beasts like him." He indicated Sutton and gave Violet a smile.

"I thank you ever so much for your kindness, Mr. Landers," Violet said.

"I thank you too, Landers," Sutton echoed. Then, to Violet, he said, "I'd best be on my way."

"Thank you again, Luke, for everything."

Sutton nodded. "Landers, you look after the lady for me."

"I'll do that," Landers promised. "This way, Miss Wilson."

As Landers led Violet into the room off the kitchen, Sutton started for the door. Just before he reached it, Violet called his name. When he turned to face her, she said, "Do be careful, Luke."

That night, after arriving back in Bailey, Sutton parked the buggy he had rented and went into the saloon where he asked the bar dog to tell him anything he could about Talbot whom he described to the man.

"Tell you what?" asked the bar dog belligerently. "You the law or something?"

"Nope, I'm not the law. I am though a man who has one helluva temper that tends to flare when he's thwarted, so I suggest you tell me what you know about Talbot and tell it all to me just as fast as ever you can." Sutton ostentatiously let his hand come to rest on the butt of his forty-five.

The bar dog stepped back, colliding with the shelf behind him and causing the bottles on it to clink against one another. "He was in here yesterday afternoon. He was trail-dusty. I took him for a drifter. After he'd had a few drinks, he got real talkative—about women mostly and how they weren't to be trusted or tamed. Said he had himself a woman, only she was being seduced by another man and was way too weak-willed to resist this other fellow's advances. He—you say his name's Talbot?—well, Talbot said he'd come to town to settle his lady friend's hash once and for all. I asked him what he intended to do. All he did was grit his teeth at first. But then he had another drink and declared he was going to kill her and her boyfriend both."

"I reckon you heard the shooting that started right after Talbot left here yesterday."

"Oh, my Lord, yes, I surely did! Saw the gunfight too. Talbot fired at this man and woman—they must have been his lady friend and her paramour—and then that man grabbed a gun from a passerby and shot back."

"Then what happened?"

"Talbot, he ran that way—" the bar dog pointed through the window—"and the other fellow went high-heeling it after him. Both of them shot out of sight up there by the parlor house."

"What else did you see?"

"Nothing after that. I had thirsty customers to see to."

Sutton turned and left the saloon. He walked to the parlor house the bar dog had pointed out to him where he knocked on the front door which was opened almost at once by a portly middle-aged woman who gave him a welcoming smile.

"I'm not here to do business," he told her and her smile vanished. "I'm looking for anybody who can tell me what happened to the two fellows who were shooting at each other in the street yesterday afternoon."

"High spirits," declared the woman offhandedly. "Most men suffer from them. A lot of them come here to calm themselves down. It works too."

"Did you see what happened?"

"Not how it started. But I looked out the window after I heard the shots."

"And saw?" Sutton prompted.

"Two men with guns racing up this way from downtown. I locked the doors and sent my girls scurrying upstairs to hide under their beds."

"What happened to the two men?"

"The one in the lead—he was a sly one," the woman said, her smile returning. "He went around the side of the feed and grain store next door and hid in the bushes behind it. The other man hunted for him for a while and then, when he didn't find him, he gave up and started back down the street. That's when the first fellow made his mistake."

"What mistake did he make?"

"He broke and ran. The other man saw him go into the livery and he started running after him again."

"Did he catch the first fellow?"

The woman shook her head. "The first one came galloping out of the livery and rode out of town. I wouldn't be surprised if he's in California by now, he was traveling that fast."

"I'm obliged to you." Sutton touched the brim of his hat to the woman.

"Honey, you come on back here when you've got spending money on your mind. My girls will be thrilled to see such a good-looking cuss as yourself and I personally guarantee you that the one you pick will give you extra-special service."

"I thank you for the compliment, ma'am," Sutton said, grinning as he left.

He returned to where he had left the buggy and returned it to the livery where he asked the liveryman about Talbot.

"He was the one who was here yesterday," the liveryman said when Sutton had finished describing Talbot to him. "Like you said, his horse had one walleye."

"I'm wondering, did he say anything to you when he first brought his horse in here or before he left here yesterday afternoon?"

"No, I don't think so," the liveryman replied, scratching his stubbled chin. "Wait. He did say one thing that I recall."

Sutton waited, trying to hide his impatience.

"He said he'd come to town to take care of some business, and when he had taken care of it, he meant to head back to someplace where there was a woman he had designs on."

"Did he mention her name?"

"He did. He said her name was Alice. He called her 'Sweet Alice.' "

"Did another man come in here right after the one I asked you about left?" Sutton described Aaron Endicott to the liveryman.

"He did and he bought a horse—a roan—from me. Didn't quibble about the price neither. Paid top dollar for the horse and the same for a saddle and bridle to put on him. He took off then like the devil himself was on his backtrail."

"I need a horse."

The liveryman frowned. "You've got a horse, mister— that dun you brought in a little while ago."

"That animal needs rest. I damn near rode him to death getting here. I need another one—a fresh one. What have you got?"

"I got one I can let go for twenty-five dollars—that bay there." The liveryman pointed to a horse in a nearby stall.

Sutton quickly examined it. When he was satisfied that the animal was sound, he paid the liveryman the price he had asked for and then saddled and bridled the bay.

Minutes later, as he rode out of Bailey heading west, he thought about what the liveryman had told him Talbot had said. Talbot probably figures on lying low awhile, he thought, before he has another go at Violet and Endicott. And the place he probably intends to lie low in is Helltown where he can keep company with Sweet Alice whom he told the liveryman he was fixing to visit. He sighed as he thought about the nearly day-long headstart Talbot had on him. Talbot and Endicott too, he corrected himself. They're both of them way ahead of me.

Endicott, he reasoned, must have seen which way Talbot went when he left town yesterday, since Endicott was chasing him when Talbot got his horse and left the livery. Right after that Endicott bought himself a horse. So chances are Endicott's somewhere up ahead and in between Talbot and me. Which suits me fine. If I can catch up to Endicott first, maybe I can calm him down and send him packing back to Violet. If I can do that, I'll have only Talbot to worry about.

He kneed the bay under him and it began to gallop, heading into the setting sun and the lengthening shad-

ows. Sutton rode as long as the light lasted. The he drew
rein at a spot near a stream and made camp for the night.

He was on the move again at first light. Instead of heading due west, he rode some distance to the south and then
backtrailed to the north. The sun was not yet above the
horizon when he found, a mile to the north, the two trails
that paralleled one another. They were no more than six
feet apart and it was apparent to Sutton that the riders
who had made them had not been traveling together
because the southernmost trail showed, by means of the
relative depth and positions of the horse's hoofprints, that
the animal was galloping and had a rider. The other trail
Sutton deduced from the placement of that horse's hoofprints showed that that horse also had a rider who was
traveling more slowly.

Talbot, he thought, staring down at the southernmost
trail. And he was in a helluva hurry. The other trail might
be Endicott's. He set out to follow them both.

As the sun rose red in the east behind him, Sutton rode
along a ridge and then down into a shallow valley. On
both sides of him, hills rose and dipped like waves of a
frozen sea. Trees speckled the slopes to which puffs of
white clouds seemed to cling.

He spotted a snow-splattered cougar upslope from him
where patches of snow could be seen. The big cat stopped
and stared down at him for a moment before moving
lithely on and finally disappearing as it topped a snowy
peak.

When Sutton came to a wide stream that had its source
some distance away where a waterfall shimmered its way
down from a mesa-like stretch of rimrock, he drew rein
and sat his saddle, staring down at the two trails he had
been following, both of which had entered the stream. He
dismounted and strode into the stream, shielding his eyes
against the glare of the sun on the water as he examined

the bottom of the stream. Stones had been overturned and the bottom was badly torn up. He left the water, mounted the bay, and forded the stream.

He rode along its bank, first in one direction, then in the other, but could find no place where either rider had emerged from the water. Talbot may have spotted Endicott on his backtrail, he thought, and set out to give Endicott the slip. He did, that is, if I've got the sign I found so far figured out right.

He was about to resume his examination of the western bank of the stream in an effort to pick up one or both of the trails he had been following when a voice that came from behind him barked, "I've got a gun aimed straight at you. Throw down your gun."

Sutton recognized the voice. "Don't shoot me. Let's talk."

"You heard what I said. Throw down your gun or I'll drill you."

Sutton slowly turned his bay until he was facing Aaron Endicott who was standing at the edge of a grove of lodgepole pines, a Smith and Wesson forty-four in his hand.

"Your gun," Endicott said, gesturing with the one in his hand. "Drop it."

Sutton didn't like the wild look in Endicott's eye. He noted the way Endicott was sweating profusely although the morning air was still cool. He drew his forty-five and dropped it to the ground. But the wild look didn't leave Endicott's eyes as a result of what he had done.

"When I found out you were following me," Endicott said, "I made up my mind to stop you."

"Now that's a funny thing," Sutton said placidly. "I had the same thing in mind—stopping *you.*"

"Well, you're not going to. I'm going to get Talbot, and when I do, I'm going to kill him."

"I know what happened back in Bailey, Endicott. I'd been trailing Talbot as you know, only I lost him. He beat me back to Bailey where you two tried to put holes in each other day before yesterday."

"Violet told you?"

"She did."

"Why are you following me?"

"To try to talk some sense into you—at Violet's request."

"I won't be talked out of killing Talbot."

"Have you given any thought to the sorry fact that he might kill you before you can do for him?"

"I intend to see to it that that doesn't happen."

"You sound like you've turned into a regular gunslinger almost overnight." Sutton took a casual step forward.

Endicott stepped quickly backward. "Don't try anything. I told you I'll not be stopped—not by you, Luke, not by Talbot, not by anybody."

"Did you spot Talbot during your travels?" Sutton asked in an almost offhanded manner.

"I did. But I lost him when I got here. He rode into the water and I had a hard time finding the place where he came out. Just about the time I did, I spotted you heading in this direction, so I hid in these pines behind me and waited for you to get here."

"What are you planning on doing now that you've got the drop on me?"

Endicott, Sutton noticed, seemed to hesitate before he answered, "See to it that you stay out of my way from this point on."

"Does that mean you're fixing to shoot me?"

Endicott's gun hand wavered slightly.

"Before you do, Endicott, I think you ought to give me a chance to deliver the message I've got for you."

"What message?"

"Violet told me to tell you that she's about as fed up with the stunts Talbot has been pulling as you are. She told me to tell you she can see only one way out of the situation."

"One way?" Endicott asked, frowning.

"She's made up her mind to go over to Talbot's side. Mind you, she's not dancing for joy about her decision, but she figures that's the only way to call him off. You ask me, Endicott, she's doing it—or going to do it—not for her sake but for yours. I think she's decided to throw in with Talbot to try to save your life."

"I won't let her do it!" Endicott bellowed.

"How do you plan on stopping her from doing it?"

"There's only one way."

"You mean by killing Talbot?"

Endicott nodded.

"Do you think Violet's going to feel the same way about you if you wind up a murderer as she does right now when you're not one? I'll answer you that one. She won't. Oh, she'll pretend nothing's changed between you. She might even try for a time to overlook the fact that the man she loves went and gunned down another man, only in the end she won't be able to—"

Endicott interrupted Sutton with, "She'll understand. I'll explain to her that I had to do it—that I had no choice."

"She could come to hating you for what you're fixing to do. She might decide you're not a bit better than Talbot if you kill him in cold blood."

"I'll have to take my chances on that score," Endicott declared stubbornly. "What's the alternative?" he asked rhetorically. "For Violet and me to spend the rest of our lives running from a drunken madman? To risk being killed, one or both of us, at any moment by him?" Endicott shook his head.

"I'll make a deal with you," Sutton proposed. "I'll go

after Talbot. You go back to Violet and take her away somewhere—somewhere far away where Talbot will never find you."

"No deals. Besides Violet and I have already tried that, but as you know, Talbot caught up with us. No, I'm thoroughly and absolutely convinced there's only one way to end this matter."

Sutton suddenly slid out of the saddle and crouched down behind the body of his bay. At the same time, he shoved the horse toward Endicott, enabling him to retrieve his dropped gun.

"Damn you, Sutton!" Endicott roared and fired a shot that went over the bay's back.

The shot spooked the horse which promptly spun around in a tight circle. As it did so, it collided with Sutton, knocking him to the ground.

As the bay continued to prance nervously next to him, Sutton tried to scramble out of its way. He had almost succeeded in doing so but then an obviously alarmed Endicott fired a second time.

His shot went wild, but it caused Sutton's mount to turn swiftly. Its left front hoof grazed Sutton's head a moment before the animal fled.

Sutton, as his vision blurred and searing pain seized his skull, tried desperately to hold on to his six-gun. But it fell from his hand at the same instant that an overwhelming and total darkness stripped his awareness of the world from him.

TEN

The sun was high in the sky when Sutton regained consciousness to find himself with his arms wrapped around the trunk of a tree against which his back was pressed and tied tightly.

The plight in which he found himself seemed to make the pain in his head worse. It felt like a sharp-bladed knife ripping into his brain and made it hard to concentrate. He let his head hang down but that, he soon discovered, did nothing to relieve the keen pain he was experiencing. He made up his mind to ignore it—or at least try to.

He raised his head and scanned the immediate area, searching for his horse. He saw no sign of the bay. Nor was his gun on the ground where it had fallen when he lost consciousness—but his hat was.

He silently damned Endicott for leaving him unhorsed, weaponless, and tied up in the wilderness. It's a wonder, he thought, he didn't kill me and have done with it. But Endicott's no killer—at least not yet he's not. He no doubt left me here figuring somebody'd be along sooner or later to let me loose. But that could be hours from now—days even. So it looks like it's up to me to get free on my own, since I've got things to do and places to go.

He thrust out his legs which had been twisted beneath him and placed the toe of his left boot against the heel of his right boot and began to try to pry the latter from his foot. Minutes later it fell to the ground and so did the knife he carried in it. He stretched out his right foot, and by twisting and turning it, succeeded in moving the bowie knife toward him. When it lay on the ground next to his pelvis, he drew his legs up under him and then slowly rose, his tied hands scraping against the tree trunk's rough bark as he did so.

Once he was upright, he carefully positioned his left foot directly in front of the knife. Then, easing his left foot forward and keeping his eyes on the knife, he kicked backward.

His left heel hit the hilt of the bowie and sent it flying along the ground to disappear behind the trunk of the tree. He turned his head and saw it lying less than a foot beyond the tree. He eased his body down along the tree trunk until he was once again sitting on the ground. Then he shifted his body to the right and reached for the bowie.

Because he could not see what he was doing, even though he turned his head as far to both the right and the left as he possibly could, he was forced to grope blindly for the knife. For long tense minutes, it eluded his grasp. But at the end of that time, his fingers finally touched its cold blade. They clawed at it, slowly drawing the knife closer to the tree. When the fingers of his right hand at last closed on the knife's hilt, he momentarily relaxed, letting the breath he had been holding out in a sibilant rush.

He maneuvered the knife until he had a good grip on its hilt and had its blade pointing toward the tree. Then, slowly and with dogged determination, he began to work on the rope that held him prisoner. He had no way of knowing if his efforts were producing results, since he could not see what he was doing. But he kept at it, unwilling to give up, while the sweat began to bead on his face and then to run in rivulets down it.

A moment later, he lost his grip on the knife and it fell from his hand.

He swore and began again to try to retrieve it. When he

had it in his hand once more, he continued working on the rope. As he did so, he also pulled on the rope with his free left hand, trying hard to sunder it.

More minutes passed, how many he had no way of knowing, although he did know that each of them seemed to him as long as any hour. He pulled even harder on the rope when he thought he felt it give slightly and sawed relentlessly away at it with the bowie.

He leaped to his feet as he finally succeeded in severing the rope, brandishing the knife in his hand like a banner of victory held high above his head.

But his silent celebration was short-lived, done to death by the sharp slivers of pain his exultant movements had sent stabbing through his skull. He reached up and gingerly touched his left temple where the bay's hoof had struck him. He found the spot swollen and thickly crusted with blood.

He bent down, retrieved his boot, put it on, and placed his bowie back inside it. He walked over to where his hat was lying on the ground and picked it up. As he clapped it back on his head, he recalled Endicott's remark about having located the spot where Talbot had come out of the stream. With that information in mind, he began to walk along the bank of the stream, determined this time to find the spot that Endicott had found earlier.

He spent the next hour and a half ranging up and then down the western bank of the stream without finding what he was looking for. It was not until he began retracing his original route that he noticed a pair of footprints about twenty yards from the bank, footprints he had not seen when he had passed the same spot earlier because then he had been concentrating on the water's edge where he had been expecting to see sign of where Talbot had emerged from the water.

He went up to the stretch of soft loam that bordered a

dense stretch of grassland and hunkered down to examine the prints for a moment before rising and examining the grass just beyond them. He bent down and picked up a branch that revealed by the sap still oozing from its severed end and its withering leaves that it had recently been torn from a tree.

Hunkering down again, he ran his fingers lightly over the loam and smiled as he made out the prints of a horse's hooves which were hidden beneath a thin layer of dirt.

No wind blew that dirt around like that, he thought as he stared at the prints that had been left, he believed, by Talbot's horse. Somebody broke off this branch and used it to try to cover up this trail, he told himself. And that somebody, who forgot to cover up two of his own footprints, goes by the name of Aaron Endicott or I miss my best guess. Studying the tangled grass that was almost as high as his thighs, he was easily able to pick out the path Talbot—if indeed it had been Talbot—had taken as he left the loam and rode into the grass. Some of the grass had fully recovered from the trampling it had received but enough of its stalks remained partially bent to reveal to an eye as keen as Sutton's where a rider had recently passed.

He dropped the branch he was holding and set out on foot across the vast grassland in pursuit of his quarry who, he hoped, would turn out to be Talbot although he knew there was no way to be sure that Talbot was the man he was now trailing. But all the evidence, he thought, points to the fact that Endicott tried to hide the trail he had found so he must have been sure it was Talbot's and wanted to make sure that I didn't find it.

And I damn near didn't. It was more good luck than good management that I just happened to spot those two footprints of Endicott's so far away from where I'd taken my first try at tracking.

As he walked on, he tried not to think about the head

start Endicott, not to mention Talbot, had on him. But he couldn't help being keenly aware of the advantage both men had over a man like himself—an ungunned and unhorsed one—who was of necessity pursuing them on foot.

Because of his disquieting thoughts, he began to lope along the trail in the hot sun which was wringing sweat from his body. He was surprised to find that the trail swerved to the north instead of heading due west as he had fully expected it to do. He began to wonder if Talbot had changed his mind about heading back to Helltown. Maybe, he speculated, Talbot spotted Endicott on his backtrail and set out to try to shake him—or at least mislead him as to where he was actually headed.

It was late afternoon when Sutton heard the sound of a shot fired from somewhere up ahead of him. He came to a sudden halt and stood without moving for a moment, listening, his eyes on the heavily forested and hilled land that lay directly ahead of him. Then he began to run again, moving among the trees to keep from being seen.

As he approached the crest of a hill, he dropped to the ground and peered over it to avoid skylining himself. He stared down at the two men and three horses far below him. He watched Talbot, who was wearing the red-banded straw hat and canvas duster that had belonged to the man in the saloon in Helltown with whom he had changed clothes, dismount and walk over to Endicott who was lying on the ground near the roan he had been riding. He stiffened as Talbot put out a foot and turned Endicott's limp body over so that it lay faceup on the ground. His glance flicked to his own horse which stood not far from Endicott's and then back to Endicott. He spotted his .45 in Endicott's waistband.

His hand went for his bowie. Withdrawing the knife from his boot, he began to run around the side of the hill, intending to try to take Talbot by surprise. When he

turned and began to run down the hill into the valley
below him, he lost his footing as a patch of gravelly ground
gave way under him. He went tumbling down the hill, his
arms flailing, his hat falling off, the world kaleidoscoping
crazily in front of his eyes.

When he struck the trunk of a tree at the bottom of the
hill, he came to a painful stop. Though dazed from his
dizzying fall, he nevertheless managed to struggle to his
feet. He stood there blinking and shaking his head as he
tried to bring his vision into focus. When he could see
clearly again, he realized that his knife was no longer in
his hand. He ran back up the hill, searching for it. It took
him several minutes but he finally found it. He scooped it
up and, on his way back down the hill, retrieved his hat
and put it on.

He was almost at the bottom of the hill again when he
heard the sound of hoofbeats. He quickened his pace, his
hand tightly gripping the bowie in his hand.

When Talbot rode into sight around the side of the hill,
Sutton raced toward him, hoping that Talbot's apparent
surprise at the sight of him would keep him from going at
once for the gun he wore in a holster strapped around his
hips. But Sutton's hope proved vain as Talbot's gun
quickly cleared leather. The man's deadly action forced
Sutton to swerve from his intended target and dive for
cover behind a low-lying hammock.

Talbot's shot missed him by a wide margin. But Sutton,
from his vantage point behind the hammock, stiffened as
Talbot slowed his mount, turned it, and headed toward
the spot where Sutton had so swiftly gone to ground.

Got to get out of here or take Talbot or both, Sutton
thought, not sure he could successfully accomplish either
task because of the determined way Talbot was stalking
him. A knife's no weapon to go up against a gun with, he
thought dismally. But it's all I have. Maybe I could . . .

He never completed his thought because Talbot spotted him and fired a shot in his direction which whined past Sutton's left ear.

Sutton sprang to his feet and threw his bowie. The knife flew through the air toward Talbot, its blade glinting brightly in the sunlight.

Talbot screamed and spun in a semicircle as Sutton's knife buried itself in his right bicep. Clutching the hilt of the knife, Talbot, still screaming, ripped it from his flesh and dropped it.

Sutton was up and running toward Talbot, determined to take advantage of his adversary's plight. But Talbot, when he saw Sutton coming at him, swiftly shifted his six-gun to his left hand. Dropping down on one knee and propping his left wrist up on his bent knee, he took aim at Sutton.

But before Talbot could fire, Sutton was on him in a flying leap. Both men went down and rolled over. Talbot screamed again as his wounded arm was buried beneath the bulk of his body. Sutton seized Talbot's left wrist and slammed it against the ground. His maneuver had the desired effect. The gun fell from Talbot's hand.

Sutton reached out, grabbed it, and got to his feet. He stood triumphantly over Talbot aiming the gun in his hand at Talbot who lay moaning now on the ground by his boots.

"It's over, Talbot," Sutton muttered between clenched teeth.

For a moment, Talbot did nothing but lie on the ground, clutching his bleeding right arm and breathing shallowly. Then, turning his body slightly and looking up at Sutton, he muttered something Sutton couldn't catch.

"What say, Talbot?"

"I said it's not."

For a moment, Sutton had no idea what the man meant.

It was only after Talbot had thrown the stone he had secreted in his left hand that Sutton realized Talbot had meant that it was not, as Sutton had claimed a moment ago, over.

The stone struck Sutton on the jaw, drawing blood and momentarily unbalancing him.

That moment was all that Talbot needed. Despite his knife wound and the pain it must be causing him, he got to his feet fast and made a grab for his gun which was still in Sutton's hand. When he failed at first to wrest it from Sutton, he kept trying—and the gun suddenly changed hands.

Sutton, with no weapon and knowing he had lost the battle, turned and fled. Once again he took cover, this time behind the stump of a deadfall. He lay there panting, his chest heaving, and his throat dry, wondering when Talbot's next shot would come.

When none did, he ventured a quick look around the stump—and swore volubly when he saw that Talbot had turned tail and was running for his horse. Heedless of the consequences of his action, Sutton leaped to his feet and went racing after Talbot.

Talbot must have heard him coming because he glanced back over his shoulder and then half turned and fired again at Sutton. But Sutton kept coming, and slowly —much too slowly to suit him—began to narrow the gap between himself and Talbot. But before he could reach his quarry, Talbot had climbed aboard his horse, kneed it, and gone galloping across the valley, swinging around in the saddle as he did so and firing one last shot at Sutton which, like his others, missed.

Sutton slowed, came to a halt. He stood there, his arms hanging by his sides, and cursed the feeling of helplessness that had taken possession of him as Talbot disappeared around a distant bend. Then he hurried over to where his bloody bowie lay on the ground. He picked it up, wiped it clean on some thatch, and returned it to his boot.

He ran back to where he had last seen Edicott, intending to repossess his gun and bay and head out after Talbot with Edicott's body thrown over his horse's withers. When he reached the spot, he was surprised to find that Endicott was inexplicably coatless. As he reached down to pick Endicott up, he drew back, startled, as Endicott suddenly rose to an unsteady sitting position, the Smith and Wesson he had taken from the stranger in Bailey during his and Violet's encounter with Talbot held loosely in his trembling right hand.

Sutton sighed and raised his hands.

Endicott fainted.

Sutton made a grab for Endicott's dropped gun. When he had it in his hand, he removed his own gun from Endicott's waistband and holstered it. Then, holding Endicott's gun on the unconscious man, he nudged him with the toe of his boot.

Endicott moaned and his eyes eased open. He stared apprehensively up at Sutton, trying to speak, but apparently unable to. Then, taking a deep breath he managed to whisper, "I don't blame you for what you're going to do to me."

"I'm not going to shoot you if that's what you mean," Sutton said. "Though I ought to an account of all the woe you've caused me."

"You're not going to shoot me?" Endicott asked incredulously as he tried to sit up only to fall back in a helpless heap.

"Don't keep pressing me on the point," Sutton muttered, "or I'm liable to change my mind and let light through you." He thrust Endicott's gun into his waistband

and then helped Endicott sit up. "I see Talbot's already done that favor for you."

"I caught up with him," Endicott wheezed as Sutton hunkered down beside him to help support him. "We exchanged some shots. I missed. Talbot didn't.

"I played dead and my ruse worked. It was hard to pull off because of the pain. Especially when he rolled me over and removed my coat. I wondered then and I'm wondering now why he took my coat. It was all bloody. And there was nothing of value in its pockets—no money—nothing."

"I can venture a guess on that score. Maybe you know that the deputy marshals in Indian Territory are in the habit of taking the boots from a fugitive they kill to prove that they got their man. My guess is that Talbot took your blood-soaked coat to show to Violet so that she'd think he'd done you in same as he thinks he did."

Endicott gasped. "What you say, Sutton—it makes sense. Talbot headed east after he took my coat. He must be on his way back to Violet."

"Whoa!" Sutton said as Endicott tried unsuccessfully to get to his feet. "You fainted once from lack of blood. Don't push your luck."

"Why are you helping me after the way I've treated you? If I were in your position, I wouldn't be half as charitable."

"Let's just say I was paid good money to see to it that you stayed in one piece and that's what I'm doing. Now let's have a look at the damage Talbot did to you."

Sutton helped Endicott remove his shirt and then he examined the two bullet wounds in Endicott's left side. "They look a lot worse than they are. The round went right through here"—he pointed to the small entry hole—"and out back here." He indicated the larger exit hole which was surrounded by torn and ragged flesh. Both wounds were crusted with dried blood, and as flies gathered and tried to settle on them, Sutton chased them away by waving Endicott's shirt at them. "You're a lucky man, Endicott. If the hit had been a little more to your right you'd have gotten it right in the gut and there'd be no hope for you. As it is, I can probably patch you up enough to get you back to Bailey."

Sutton rose and left Endicott. When he returned some time later, he was carrying a handful of moss and his canteen which he had filled at a creek near the spot where he had gathered the moss.

He hunkered down beside Endicott and proceeded to rip the right sleeve from the man's shirt which he then soaked with water. He swabbed both of Endicott's wounds, freeing them of their newly formed scabs. When Endicott protested, saying he had already lost too much blood, Sutton countered with, "It's an old Indian trick. Set the blood to running if you want to clean out a wound. Keeps it from getting infected that way."

When he was satisfied that both wounds were clean, he packed them with moss and then used the wet shirt sleeve he had been using as a sponge as a bandage which he wrapped and tied around Endicott's waist.

"That ought to hold you all together for the time being anyway," he remarked when he had finished his task. "Now comes the hard part."

"What you just did—I thought *that* was the hard part," Endicott quipped with a feeble attempt at a smile. "You'd never make a doctor, Sutton. You've got an awful bedside manner. Not to mention hard hands."

"I got to get you up on your horse," Sutton said. "You ready to give it a try?"

"I guess I'm as ready as I ever will be although I'm not making you any promises about whether or not I can get aboard my mount, let alone stay in the saddle."

"You're going to do both on account of you've got to.

I've got to get to Violet before Talbot does and I can't just leave you behind out here with only the wolves and turkey buzzards for company. Let's go."

Sutton helped Endicott to his feet. He placed Endicott's right arm over his shoulders and then, gripping the man around the waist with one arm and holding Endicott's wrist in his other hand, he helped him over to his horse.

Endicott made it into the saddle of the roan on his third try, causing Sutton to remark dryly, "Folks say the third time's the charm."

"Do you think we can reach Violet before Talbot does?" Endicott asked edgily. "He's got a head start on us."

"I'd say we have a better than fair chance to," Sutton replied. "Talbot will be heading due east for Bailey and we'll be heading back to the logging camp."

"Why go to the logging camp when Violet's at the hotel in Bailey?"

"She's not. I took her up to the camp and left her with the cook, Landers, in case Talbot got the notion to come back after her as it appears he's now on his way to do. He's in for a surprise when he gets to Bailey and finds her gone. While he's stymied in town, we'll have gotten to her."

"Then we had better hurry," Endicott declared and started to move his horse out.

Sutton put out a hand to steady him as Endicott slumped to one side. "I can tie your feet together under your mount's belly," he said, "and your hands to your saddle horn if you think that'll help you stay in the saddle."

"I can manage," Endicott insisted.

"Then let's ride," Sutton said and swung into the saddle of his bay.

The journey to the logging camp took Sutton and Endicott almost twice as long as it should have because of

Endicott's poor condition. Twice Sutton had to stop along the trail to let the man rest and both of those times—and at other times as well—he had refused to listen to Endicott's orders and pleas to leave him and travel on alone because he believed that if he abandoned Endicott the man might not make it back to civilization. If that belief proved to be true, he felt he would have failed to do what Violet Wilson had hired him to do. In addition, he would have failed, he felt, to be a friend to a man in desperate need of one.

Sutton's spirits, which had been dulled by worry over the possible fate of Violet, lifted when he rode with Endicott past several teams of buckers and fallers working on the western edge of the logging camp's preserve. Some of the men, recognizing him and Endicott, waved.

"I can't wait to see her," Endicott told Sutton, his eyes aglow. "I'm going to take her in my arms and hug the daylights out of her and then I'm going to scoop her up and run off with her as fast as my feet will carry me."

"The way you talk makes me think your wounds must have got infected after all even with the care I gave them," Sutton said with a smile. "That sounds to me a lot like fever talk."

"I suppose it does and I suppose it is in a way," Endicott agreed as they rode through a cleared portion of the forest where the stumps of trees sprouted like stiff mushrooms. "What is love if not a kind of fever?"

Later, as they rode into the camp which appeared to be deserted, Sutton held up a hand and drew rein.

"Is something wrong?" Endicott asked apprehensively.

Sutton scanned the campground but saw nothing amiss. "Violet's staying in a room in back of the dining hall." He heeled his horse and walked it in the direction of the dining hall, Endicott riding at his side.

Endicott, despite the pain his wounds still gave him, got

quickly out of the saddle and headed for the closed door of the dining hall.

Sutton was about to dismount when movement off to his extreme right caught his eyes. He turned his head in that direction and then ordered Endicott to halt. When Endicott didn't, Sutton repeated the order without raising his voice any more than was necessary to be heard. This time Endicott, after obeying his order, turned and asked, "What is it?"

Sutton pointed.

Endicott looked to his left and saw the gray horse with the one walleye that had ambled into sight as it devoured what browse it could find growing on the side of the dining hall.

"That's Talbot's mount," Sutton explained.

"But you said he wouldn't be able to find out that Violet was here."

"If I said that, I was wrong, looks like. Endicott, you get yourself away from that there door. Hightail it around behind this building and find out if it has a back window. Then come back here and tell me what you found. Mind you, walk soft and don't let yourself be seen."

"You think he's in there—Talbot? With Violet?"

"How the hell do I know? I can't see through walls or read minds." Sutton immediately regretted the words he had snapped at Endicott which were, he realized, the result of his growing fears that he was in danger of losing not just the battle with Talbot he had already lost back along the trail but also the entire war. "Get a move on, Endicott!" he ordered, his tone still harsh.

As Endicott disappeared around the side of the dining hall, Sutton dismounted and made his way to the front door of the hall. He positioned himself to one side of it, his back against the wall of the building. Reaching out, he got a grip on the doorknob and slowly turned it. Easing the door open, he stood there, straining to hear whatever might be going on inside.

He heard muffled voices—a man's and a woman's.

Endicott returned and reported in a voice too loud to suit Sutton, "There's no back door. No back window either."

"Quiet down!" Sutton ordered.

"You hear something? See anything?"

Instead of answering, Sutton pulled Endicott's gun from his waistband and asked, "Can I trust you not to shoot me if I turn this over to you?"

"You know I wouldn't—"

"Take it. I'm going inside. If Talbot should happen to come out this door on the run, stop him. If you can't stop him, shoot him. You got that?"

Endicott nodded.

Sutton gave the door a slight shove and it swung inward. He leaned around the side of the jamb and peered into the dim interior of the dining hall. He saw no one. But he could still hear the two voices although he could not understand any of the words being spoken. He eased inside and then hurried toward the entrance to the kitchen at the rear of the building where the voices were coming from.

At its door, he halted, listening, and was able to identify the voices he heard as Talbot's and Violet's. He silently swore as he heard Violet say, "Oh, how I damn the day I told the desk clerk in the hotel in Bailey that I was coming here."

"I don't," Sutton heard Talbot respond gleefully. "I could have wasted weeks tracking you down if you hadn't left me such a plain trail. I—"

"You stand where you are, Talbot, and drop that gun," Sutton commanded as he stepped into the kitchen with the revolver in his hand aimed at Talbot's gut.

When Talbot went for his gun, Sutton put a bullet into the wall on his right. The warning shot worked. Talbot's hand flew away from his gun.

"Drop it!" Sutton ordered.

Talbot's hand eased back down toward his revolver. Slowly he unleathered it. Quickly he aimed it at Violet who was standing only two feet away from him. Then he sprang toward her, put one arm around her waist, and pressed the muzzle of his weapon against her temple as he stood behind her. "Now what move do you have in mind, Sutton?" he taunted.

Sutton met Violet's terrified gaze and then looked back at Talbot. "This is between you and me, Talbot," he snapped. "Let the lady go."

"Not on your life will I let her go, Sutton," Talbot responded. "She's my high card and now that you've shown up again to pester me some more, I'm playing her. Move away from that door."

When Sutton was slow to comply with the order, Talbot tightened his grip on Violet, causing her to emit a strangled cry and Sutton to step away from the door.

Talbot, half dragging Violet with him, circled warily around Sutton. "Don't you come after me," he snarled. "You do and the lady here's dead. Same as her fiancée is."

"Luke, he killed Aaron!" Violet wailed and tears filled her eyes. "He brought me Aaron's coat to prove it. It's over there."

Sutton didn't look in the direction she was pointing, keeping his eyes fastened instead on Talbot's face as he waited for the man to make a wrong move that would give him the chance to—

"You don't want me to have to kill the lady like I did her fiancée, do you, Sutton?" Talbot sneered.

"No, Talbot, I don't."

"Then do what you're told. Don't follow me. If you do, you and her both will pay for your foolishness."

Talbot left the kitchen and hurried with Violet across the broad expanse of the dining hall. Sutton, from the kitchen doorway, watched him go, hoping that Endicott would now be able to do what he had failed to do—stop Talbot—but doubting that possibility even as he thought of it.

He stiffened with tense anticipation as Talbot dragged Violet through the open dining hall door and outside.

He heard her cry out as he ran toward the door. By the time he reached it, Talbot was in the saddle with Violet thrown face down over his horse's withers.

Sutton, noting the stricken look on Endicott's drawn face, knew there was no need to warn him not to try to take Talbot. When Endicott lowered his gun and gave him a pleading look, Sutton muttered more to himself than to Endicott, "It's a Mexican standoff if I ever saw one."

"We have to do something," Endicott groaned.

But it was Talbot who did something. He fired twice in rapid succession and before the smoke had cleared both Sutton's bay and Endicott's roan lay dying on the ground and Talbot was galloping toward the forest.

Sutton, helplessly watching him go, swore aloud, giving vent to his frustration.

"He's getting away!" Endicott wailed helplessly as Talbot disappeared among the trees. "And we can't follow him. Not with two dead horses, we can't."

"I can," Sutton said as an idea suddenly occurred to him.

Endicott gave him an incredulous look. "How?"

"You stay put right here. Don't try to follow me. You'll not be able to handle what I have in mind to do, not shot up the way you are, you won't."

Sutton holstered his gun and began to run in the direction Talbot had taken, passing Kemp who was driving his wagon, which was fully loaded with supplies, into camp. He could hear the sound of Talbot's horse as it went crashing through the forest up ahead of him and he could also hear Violet's cries as she was being borne unwillingly away by Talbot. But a few minutes later, both sounds gave way to the stillness of the forest. Sutton raced on until he reached the flume which was filled with rushing water.

He yelled to a man standing in the doorway of a flume tender's shack on the far side of the flume. When he had the man's attention, he asked where he could find a flume boat.

"I've got one inside," the flume tender called back. "What do you want it for?"

"Got to get myself down the mountain in a hurry." Sutton ducked under the flume between its supporting wooden uprights and took the boat the flume tender handed him with an "Obliged."

He took one look at the roaring water which was not at the moment carrying any logs down its twisting course and then climbed up on one of the uprights.

"You sure you know what you're doing?" the flume tender asked him as he watched Sutton lower the boat toward the water.

Sutton hoped he did. All he knew for sure was that the instant he realized Talbot and Violet were heading straight down the mountain after leaving the logging camp an image of the flume which also headed in that direction had flashed through his mind. He recalled Endicott's earlier description of how an injured man had been sent down the flume on a flume boat so he could receive medical attention at the foot of the mountain.

Sutton placed the boat in the water, held it in place, and then dropped down upon it. Instantly he was borne down the flume at a rapidly increasing pace, the wooden sides of the V-shaped boat bumping noisily against the wooden sides of the U-shaped trough of the flume.

Water splashed up all around him, wetting his body, face, and clothes. He braced his boots against the keel of the tiny boat. Wind shrilled in his ears. Half-glimpsed images of towering trees, snow-topped peaks, and granite hills fled past his eyes and were gone. As the flume turned and twisted its snake-like way down the mountain, Sutton found himself holding on for dear life while thinking grimly that what he was doing felt like riding the milltails of hell.

The landscape whizzing past his dazzled eyes began to blur as his speed increased. His body shifted from side to side as the boat followed the flume's winding course, leaning first one way, then the other. He held his breath as the flume flew out onto a seemingly sky-high trestle, feeling as he traversed as if he were suspended in midair.

He wiped the wet spray from his eyes, thinking, I've not got too much farther to go. It's up ahead here somewheres as I remember. He squinted through the spray shimmering in the sunlight as the boat bearing him careened onward and downward at head-spinning speed.

There!

He finally saw what he had been looking for during the preceding seconds—the place he had seen earlier when he had been working as a flume tender where a section of the side of the flume had been removed to permit logs to fly out of the flume and pile up on the ground to await wagons that would haul them away. His blood began to drum in his head. His eyes were on the slatted and upwardly angled wedge of wood that raised the logs and let them go shooting out of the opened wall of the flume without any loss of water.

Here I go, he thought, tensing.

As the flume boat met the inclined wedge, its keel rose and then, as it angled upward along the slatted wooden ledge, it shot out into space, seeming to hang suspended there for one heart-stopping moment before beginning to drop precipitously downward. Sutton tightly gripping both sides of the boat, resisting the impulse both to close his eyes and to pray.

Closing his eyes, he reasoned, might make matters worse. Better, he told himself, to see whatever was coming. Praying, he was convinced, would not alter his headlong course which was ruled by awesome physical forces and not the whims of any deity he had ever heard of.

The flume boat struck a tall pile of logs and shattered into two pieces. As Sutton was thrown from it, his body hit the logs and for a moment he felt and knew nothing. A moment later, however, his senses returned to him and he realized he was rolling down the pile of logs to the ground below. When he came to a halt, he lay without moving for several minutes, wondering if he had broken anything, hoping he hadn't, glad he was still alive.

He sighed with relief as he got to his feet in one unbroken piece. But his body was racked by painful bruises and he was completely drenched. He took a deep breath and looked around. Then he loped over to a stand of sugar pines and took cover within them, hoping as he did so that Talbot had not changed his course, that the man was still headed straight down the mountain with his captive, his route still, as it had when it began back at the logging camp, paralleling the course of the flume.

Sutton waited, his gun drawn. He listened for the sound of an approaching rider but none reached his ears. But that was a real fast flume ride I took, he reminded himself, not just a wet one. That little boat must have scooted down the flume at close to—or maybe over—a hundred miles an hour. So I probably bypassed Talbot a long ways back.

Still, as more minutes passed with still no sign of Talbot, Sutton began to worry. He dropped to his hands and knees and placed his left ear against the ground. When at last he heard the sound of hoofbeats pounding the ground, he sprang to his feet and, taking cover behind a sugar pine, stared in the direction from which he expected Talbot to appear at any moment.

When Talbot rode into sight and headed toward him with Violet still draped over the gray's withers, Sutton stepped out from behind the pine tree, leveled his six-gun at the man, and ordered him to halt.

But Talbot didn't. Instead, he kneed his horse and sent it galloping straight at Sutton.

Knowing that what he was about to do might endanger Violet but knowing also that there was no other way to stop Talbot short of killing him, Sutton took careful aim and shot Talbot's walleyed mount right between the eyes.

The horse dropped like a stone, sending Talbot and Violet rolling head over heels in different directions.

Wasting no time, Sutton sprinted out into the open. He positioned himself protectively between Talbot and Violet and ordered Talbot to get to his feet.

But Talbot, ignoring the order, went for his gun instead. Sutton shot him.

Then, as Talbot, wounded in the right shoulder but still alive because Sutton had deliberately aimed where he had in order to wound but not to kill his antagonist, prepared to squeeze off another shot, Sutton threw himself to the ground. From a prone position with his gun held steady in both hands he fired again, killing Talbot this time with a round that blew away most of the man's lower jaw as it burned its deadly way up into his brain.

As Talbot's knees buckled and he went down, Sutton

rose. He stared down at the dead Talbot for a long moment and then, holstering his smoking .45, turned to Violet who still lay where she had fallen, one hand covering her mouth as she stared in horrified fascination at Talbot's corpse. He went over to her and helped her to her feet. "You hurt?" he asked her.

She slowly shook her head. "He's dead, isn't he?"

"He's dead."

"I didn't want it to end this way. I didn't want Dade to die."

"I had to kill him. The first time I just wounded him on purpose. But he wouldn't stop trying to kill me. So I shot him again to save my own hide."

"Oh, I know, Luke," Violet cried. "I didn't mean what I said to sound like criticism of you. I saw what happened— what you did and what Dade did. I fully realize that you acted in self-defense."

Violet hesitated and then continued, "Dade told me he killed Aaron, Luke. And yet, when he dragged me out of the dining hall, I thought—there was a man out there—I caught just a glimpse of him—I thought he was Aaron. I guess that's because I didn't want to believe that Dade had killed Aaron, so I imagined the man I saw was him. What wicked tricks one's heart can play on one."

"The man you saw, Violet—that was Aaron."

"It was— But Dade told me he had shot and killed Aaron."

"Talbot shot him all right but he didn't kill him. Endicott played possum and Talbot left him for dead. I found him and patched him up and brought him back to the logging camp. He was going to try to take Talbot, if he could, the same as me. But when Talbot got his hands on you, there was nothing either Endicott or I could do."

"Oh, Luke, how can I ever thank you for saving Aaron for me?"

"No need to. I'm just glad I was able to do what you sent me out to do."

"Luke, let's hurry back to the camp. I can't wait to see Aaron again."

Later, when they arrived at the camp, Violet left Sutton and went racing toward Endicott who was standing in front of the dining hall talking to Kemp, the camp's supplier, whose wagon had been emptied of supplies. When Endicott saw her coming toward him, he left Kemp and ran to meet her.

By the time Sutton had joined them, they were locked in an emotional embrace. When they separated, Endicott, his eyes on Sutton, asked, "Where's Talbot?"

Sutton told him what had happened farther down the mountain.

Violet said, "Aaron, on the way up here Luke told me everything that happened. About Dade shooting you and about his flume ride—"

"Flume ride?" Endicott inquired of Sutton.

Sutton explained and then, "I'm going over to have a talk with Kemp, see if I can get a ride into Bailey on his wagon where I can pick up my dun at the livery there and then head back to Virginia City."

Violet and Endicott conferred briefly in hushed tones and then she turned to Sutton and said, "With Dade no longer a threat to Aaron and me, Luke, we've decided to return to Virginia City and take up our lives there again. Do you think that gentleman over there—I believe you said his name was Kemp—would allow us to ride to Bailey in his wagon with you?"

"Kemp's an agreeable old codger. I'm sure he'll take us all into town."

"Aaron and I," Violet continued, "will buy horses there and travel with you back to Virginia City."

"That sounds fine to me."

As Violet and Endicott again embraced, Sutton, watching the lovers, found himself thinking of the lovely Cassandra Pritchett and remembering with pleasure the delights he had shared with her the night before he left Virginia City to search for Endicott.

It was because of those fond and arousing memories that he responded with an eager "So am I" to Violet's remark that she was anxious to get back to Virginia City just as fast as possible.

ABOUT THE AUTHOR

Leo P. Kelley has published seven novels in the Luke Sutton series. His most recent Double D Western is entitled *Morgan*. He lives in Long Beach, New York.